A
Harlequin
Romance

1519

OTHER

Harlequin Romances

by IRIS DANBURY

Many of these titles are available at your local bookseller,
or through the Harlequin Reader Service.

For a free catalogue listing all available Harlequin Romances,
send your name and address to:

HARLEQUIN READER SERVICE,
M.P.O. Box 707, Niagara Falls, N.Y. 14302.
Canadian address: Stratford, Ontario, Canada.

or use order coupon at back of book.

SUMMER COMES TO ALBAROSA

by

IRIS DANBURY

HARLEQUIN BOOKS

TORONTO ● **WINNIPEG**

First published in 1971 by Mills & Boon Limited,
17-19 Foley Street, London, England

SBN 373-01519-4

© Iris Danbury 1971

Harlequin Canadian edition published August, 1971
Harlequin U.S. edition published November, 1971

Printed in Canada

CHAPTER ONE

'You fly to Madrid, then change planes there for Granada. The rest you can do by car.'

It had all sounded so simple this morning when Caran left Heathrow, but now, coming in to land at Granada in the twilight of a mid-October afternoon, with only the rose-flushed tips of the Sierra Nevada outlined against the darkening sky, the prospect of that further journey to Albarosa daunted her.

After snatching a quick meal at the airport there was the difficulty of finding a car-driver to take her. She decided to stay the night in Granada and continue next day.

She approached one of the airport officials. 'Could you recommend a small hotel for one night?'

'Certainly, *señorita*.' He consulted a reference book and wrote down addresses on a slip of paper. Then as she thanked him, another official told her that he had found someone who was driving in her direction and would take her the rest of the way to Albarosa.

Outside the airport buildings a tall man stood by the car door and in the dimmed lights she caught no more than a glimpse of a lean, serious face and dark eyes.

She asked the price for the journey—'Always find out first what it costs,' she had been advised before she left England.

'I am driving to Almeria for my own purposes anyway. We can discuss the extra charge later.' She guessed by his voice that he was Spanish although he spoke excellent English.

When he saw that she still hesitated, he assured her, 'I will not overcharge you, *señorita*.'

She checked her luggage, then settled herself in the car. On the darkened road, punctuated only by occasional flashing headlights from other cars or lorries, she had time to dwell on the extraordinary circumstances that had brought her rushing along the twisting roads of Andalucia, not even

5

for a summer holiday, but in the middle of winter. More than that, in the company of a strange man whom she had not seen clearly and whose name she did not know. She had been looking for adventure, and now perhaps it was speeding towards her more rapidly than she had bargained for.

Caran Ingram had suddenly become tired of her humdrum secretarial job in the large insurance company. 'You're nothing but a number,' she complained to her flat-mate, Julie. 'If I'm not careful I shall become part of the furniture—fourth desk along the right, next to the filing cupboard.'

'Strike out into something new,' advised Julie, who struck out frequently and sometimes disastrously. 'It's fatal to be landed in a rut.'

The employment bureaux offered Caran a wide selection of posts, but few appealed to her. She was dubious about exchanging the frying pan for the fire.

'What d'you want, then?' demanded Julie one morning. 'To be secretary to a princess or a world-famous author?'

'I'm not sure that I want to go on being a secretary to anyone,' murmured Caran.

'You can't *do* anything else,' was Julie's blunt comment. After a second cup of coffee, she handed over the morning paper to Caran. 'Look down the ads. There are several interesting ones if they appeal to you. Can't stop. I must fly.'

Caran examined the advertisements. One in Switzerland, definitely secretarial, but another merely asked for a sensible young woman to manage five villas in Spain, and added a telephone number.

Caran's interview with Mrs. Parmenter, the owner of the villas, went well.

'If you're interested, I think you'd suit admirably,' this middle-aged woman told her. 'I've had such trouble and bad luck with the two previous firms of agents that were supposed to look after the villas, so I've decided to employ someone to live on the spot.'

After a long discussion about her duties and responsibilities as a kind of manager–housekeeper, Caran was convinced that the job was attractive and just what she was looking for. She had assured Mrs. Parmenter that she was entirely domesticated, having been trained by her mother. She had the extra advantage in that she had been learning Spanish at evening classes and could cope with the language even if she lacked fluency.

She would have impulsively accepted the post on the spot, but Mrs. Parmenter suggested a few days to think it over, perhaps consult her parents.

Julie was less than enthusiastic. 'Spain?' she echoed. 'That means I'll have to get someone else to share the flat. Oh, why did you let your job bore you? All you needed was a new man to take you out.'

Caran laughed at that. Every time she acquired a new man acquaintance, Julie lost no time in annexing him. Her mind was made up now for the new job, never mind the new man.

She gave her notice to the insurance company, then paid a brief visit to her parents in Gloucestershire to reassure them about taking a job in a foreign country. Back to London to collect her necessary belongings and receive final instructions from her new employer.

This morning when she had come to Heathrow to see Caran off, Mrs. Parmenter had been accompanied by her nephew, Paul, an attractive young man who said how much he envied Caran going to southern Spain at this time of year.

'Lucky you, to be escaping the English winter, but I shall be coming to Albarosa fairly soon and I shall insist that you take some time off so that I can show you some of Andalucia.'

He cast a provocative glance at his aunt, but there was no more time for conversation. Caran saw him later at the waving base as the plane slid along the runway. Julie had announced her intention of seeing Caran off, but changed her mind at the last minute as she had a lunch-date with a new man friend.

Now Caran was being driven at frightening speed by a man who seemed to pay more attention to his cigar-smoking than to his driving. A cluster of lights appeared in the distance and he slowed down a little. 'Are you hungry?' he asked politely. 'We could have something at the next town.'

Uncertain of how long it would take to arrive at Albarosa and, again, what she might find there, Caran decided to eat when the opportunity offered. 'I had very little at the airport,' she answered, 'so I'd like to stop wherever it's convenient.'

She noticed, though, that he included himself in whatever meal they might share. What was she to do now without causing this polite Spaniard embarrassment? Perhaps she could ask him to pay the bill for her and add the amount to the total fare.

When they alighted in a small square and he conducted her to a restaurant she had a clearer view of her companion. Tall and slim she had imagined him to be, but she had not noticed the proud Latin nose, the high cheekbones and hard jawline. His black hair matched his strongly marked eyebrows.

Here was no ordinary taxi-driver, and for a second or two she hesitated, but he took her elbow and guided her to a table, where he was amiably greeted by the proprietor. So evidently he was known here, unless this welcome was merely the usual Spanish smiling courtesy.

'Perhaps we had better introduce ourselves,' he said, while she studied the menu. 'My name is Ramiro Mendosa. And yours?'

A vague uneasiness caused her to hesitate. Was it essential to exchange names with a car-driver who gave you a lift because he was going in your direction?

She glanced up and caught the amused expression in his dark eyes.

'Have I offended you or have you some reason for not wanting to be known?'

'No reason at all,' she replied crisply. She must not let him imagine that she was some kind of criminal on the run. 'I'm Caran Ingram.'

'Caran,' he repeated softly. 'That is an English name unknown to me.'

'It's really Caroline Anne, but I've always been called Caran since I was small.'

He surveyed her with a frankness that she found slightly embarrassing. 'Yes, the name suits you,' he decided at last. 'Then you are not on holiday? Our tourists do not usually choose October.'

She smiled at him now. Better tell him the whole story or he would certainly extract it from her piece by piece. Yet she could not agree that it was any business of his. Once she arrived at her destination she was unlikely to see him again.

Glasses of dry *manzanilla* were brought to the table. No doubt Don Ramiro imagined that a glass of wine would surely loosen her tongue, but over the meal of grilled prawns almost six inches long, followed by a delicious helping of roast pork with mushrooms, Caran told her host why she was travelling in Spain at such an odd time of year.

'So you are working at Albarosa?' he asked.

'That's what I came for,' she replied.

'Albarosa,' he murmured. Then, after a pause, 'Do you know where these villas are?'

'Only that they're near the shore.'

'But not at all near the town.'

'Perhaps that doesn't matter to me. Do you know the place well?'

'I live just outside this town where we are now, Almeria, but yes, I could say that I know Albarosa quite well. It is not a holiday resort—at least not what I think the English would regard as such a place.'

'Maybe that's why people want to go there and stay in my employer's villas, for the sake of peace and quiet. Not everyone wants to be surrounded by crowds on beaches.'

His mouth curved in a faint smile. 'You are already defending a place you have not yet seen.'

'True,' she admitted. 'How much farther is it to Albarosa from here?'

'About a hundred kilometres,' he answered.

Her eyes widened with surprise. 'But that's about—what? —sixty miles or so. It will be very late when we arrive.'

He smiled. 'Not perhaps as late as you imagine.' He looked at his watch. 'It is still only half-past nine.'

A glance at her own watch confirmed that this was so, but

another two hours' travelling would land her at Albarosa not much before midnight.

'Yes, I see. It seems to have been dark for so long at this time of year. I thought it was later. But I can't let you drive me all that way.'

His curved eyebrows rose. 'No? Then what will you do? Try to get a taxi from here?'

'It might be possible,' she muttered lamely.

'But not desirable, *señorita*. What makes you unwilling to trust me for the rest of the journey after you have come this far?'

She realised that her objections might sound ungrateful to a man who had driven her a considerable distance and who was mindful that she needed a meal and then acted the charming host.

She gave him a half-smile, partly to reassure him that she saw the sense of accepting his escort until her destination, but partly to reassure herself that there was no alternative.

'Then if you do not mind the inconvenience, I shall be very grateful to continue with you,' she said with a touch of dignity, affected a little, perhaps, by his cool composure and acceptance of the situation.

Soon after they left the inn at Almeria, rain began to appear on the windscreen and in the headlights the road appeared like black patent leather. Don Ramiro slackened his speed slightly, for which concession she was thankful. Sitting in the front seat, she was more aware of the twists and turns of road, the occasional blinding lights from approaching vehicles.

It seemed to Caran that the journey was taking most of the night, but at last they were climbing a steep, sinuous road and she could see a few isolated lights.

'Is this Albarosa?' she asked.

He nodded.

'I hope I can find the villas,' she continued. 'I'd no idea it was going to be so dark.'

'Did you think they would be floodlit for your arrival?'

The sarcastic edge to his tone made her answer sharply. 'No, I didn't. Nor did I expect a red carpet.'

'You will not be able to reach the villas tonight, *señorita*,' he told her. 'The road out of the other side of the town ends in a rough path and tonight it will be a small river.'

'But what am I to do?' She was suddenly afraid. What had she let herself in for? In the next moment she told herself not to be stupid and babyish, believing that every unknown man in a foreign country was bent on kidnapping her. 'Is there a small inn where I could stay?' she asked, forcing her voice to a calm tone.

'I shall take you to a friend who will look after you well for the night. In the morning, you will see everything in daylight.'

He was now in the centre of a deserted town, even though a few lights streamed out from bars and occasionally a figure dashed across the street to take shelter from the torrential downpour. Then he stopped outside a tall house with a massive wooden door.

'Wait here while I go inside and make arrangements with Señora Molina,' he commanded, and leapt out agilely across the pavement. A small section of the door opened at his touch and he disappeared inside. In about five minutes he returned to the car.

'Everything is arranged,' he told her. 'You will stay with my friends for the night. Take your handbag and I will attend to the rest of your luggage.'

Even as she dashed out of the car and ran towards the door, the heavy rain attacked her and she stumbled breathlessly into what she imagined to be the house, but now she was in a wide courtyard, dimly lit, with a stairway in one corner. A plump, elderly woman came towards her.

'*Bienvenido!*' she greeted Caran, holding out both hands in welcome.

'I'm sorry to put you to so much trouble,' began Caran in her careful Spanish.

The *señora* waved away such apologies. 'I am happy to do anything for Don Ramiro.'

Caran was shepherded towards the curving stone stairway and then shown into a living room, slightly crowded with dark, solid furniture, but giving a welcome warmth to Caran who was now feeling chilled by the cold, wet evening.

'First, a glass of wine, then you must eat,' declared her hostess.

'Wine, perhaps,' agreed Caran, 'but Don Ramiro took me to dinner in Almeria.'

'But of course. He would not let you starve.'

Don Ramiro now entered the room. 'I have put your luggage downstairs in the patio,' he told Caran. 'Señora Molina, permit me to introduce to you Señorita Caran Ingram, if I have her name correct. She is from England.' To Caran he said, 'Señora Molina, who is your hostess for the night.'

Caran knew that there was no point in stressing her apologies for the trouble she was giving. Better to say thank you and leave it at that.

After the promised glass of wine and a couple of biscuits, Caran was shown to the bedroom she was to occupy.

'It is always ready for my daughter,' explained Señora Molina. 'She is a nurse in Granada and sometimes she comes without warning.' The woman laughed happily. 'But then we do not want warnings when those we love come home.'

Caran warmed to this friend of Don Ramiro. She told Señora Molina that she had come to look after the villas belonging to Señora Parmenter, but the woman looked blank.

'They are near the shore and have the names of jewels, like Villa Turquesa and Villa Cristal and so on,' explained Caran.

'Oh! Yes, yes.' The woman's face cleared, then a slightly anxious expression crossed her plump features. She turned away hastily. 'I will fetch a hot-water bottle for you.'

As Señora Molina went out, Don Ramiro appeared in the doorway. 'I brought you this bag in case you needed some of your possessions for the night.' He held out the small overnight holdall.

'Oh, thank you, Don Ramiro,' Caran said. 'That was thoughtful of you.'

He bowed slightly. 'Good night, *señorita*. I hope you sleep well and may I wish you great good luck in your task, your new career.'

When he had gone she thought he had made his good wishes sound as though she would need all the luck she could get. Was there something sinister about these villas? Or was it perhaps that they were regarded as an intrusion into an unspoilt town, one that had not yet geared itself for crowds of tourists?

All this she would have to find out tomorrow. In the meantime she was tired and immensely grateful to Don Ramiro and his friend, Señora Molina, for this comfortable room.

The high Spanish bed was covered with a heavy red and white quilt and the beautifully carved bedhead was of some dark wood that matched the rest of the furniture. Thick wool rugs with intricate patterns in blue, white and black covered the marble tiled floor and several flower paintings decorated the walls. A pleasant room for a daughter to return to, Caran thought as eventually she slid into a sound sleep that seemed to last no time at all, for Señora Molina had entered with coffee and rolls and was already drawing back the heavy curtains.

'*Buenos dias,*' called the older woman. 'The sun shines this morning after the rain.'

When Caran was dressed and ready to leave after breakfast, she said tentatively, 'If you will tell me how much I owe you, *señora*,' but the woman waved away any further words.

'Don Ramiro has settled whatever there was to settle,' she declared hastily, 'and of course, we are friends.'

Caran knew better than to insist on paying for a night's lodging. No doubt there might be other ways in the future when she could return Señora Molina's kindness.

'Don Ramiro did not stay here?' queried Caran.

The Spanish woman shrugged her plump shoulders and thrust out her hands in a gesture that indicated the wilfulness of men. 'No. He could have stayed here in a comfortable bed, but no, he must drive his car back to Almeria.'

'I see. I was sorry to give him such trouble in bringing me here.'

'Don Ramiro does not think of trouble if he can help

someone,' returned Señora Molina with some emphasis.

Caran smiled at the woman who was evidently such a staunch supporter of Don Ramiro.

'Is it far from here to the villas?' she asked, thinking of her luggage that had to be conveyed there somehow.

'Vicente—he is the son of a neighbour—he will take you and your cases when you are ready.'

Another instance of Don Ramiro's thoughtfulness, Caran supposed, and now she was slightly regretful that perhaps she would never see him again, even to thank him for his help.

She followed Vicente, a lithe young Spaniard, through the courtyard and waved goodbye to her hostess. Outside along the street she made a mental note of the name, Calle de San Pedro. Later on, she would try to take a small present or a few flowers to Señora Molina by way of thanks.

Vicente turned numerous corners, led her down side streets and eventually to a point where the cobbled roadway faded into an indeterminate path of puddles and mud strewn with large stones.

'Is this the right way?' she asked her escort.

'*Si, si, señorita,*' he assured her.

Certainly the winding path led down towards the shore and that was the right direction, but surely there must be another and better approach. Most cars would find it difficult to negotiate.

At last the path led to a tangle of bushes, oleanders and yuccas sparkling with raindrops, and a patio in front of a small villa.

Vicente dumped the cases by the front door. 'It is the villa?' he asked.

'Yes,' she answered absently. 'Thank you for bringing me here.' She handed him a twenty-peseta note which was apparently more than he had expected, and with a smile and repeated thanks, he turned and disappeared through the garden as though glad to get away.

As far as she could see there was no name on the villa, although she had been told that hers was the Villa Joyosa, the first one you came to from the road.

Well, this was the first one apparently. Mrs. Parmenter had said that an old woman, Manuela, living in a small shack near by, would hand Caran the keys of all the villas as soon as she arrived, but there was no sign of anyone waiting, and probably the woman had waited last night, but given up when the rainstorm broke.

Gingerly, Caran tried the handle of the front door and was relieved when apparently the door was unlocked. Inside, she found herself in a small hallway leading to a fairly large living room. Everywhere were signs of a very untidy occupant; books and papers littered the table, a man's donkey jacket lay across a chair, a half-full bottle of wine was dumped on the window-sill, along with a couple of oranges and a bread-knife.

This was certainly not the villa intended for her own occupation, unless some intruder had taken possession of it. Then the explanation occurred to her. Mrs. Parmenter had mentioned the one permanent tenant, a Mr. Eldridge, and this must be his villa.

Caran walked towards the front door when it occurred to her that possibly Mr. Eldridge might actually be here in the villa. He might be ill, unable to look after himself.

She turned back and knocked at what might be a bedroom door. 'Anyone at home?' she called in English, then in Spanish. When no one answered she opened the door a few inches and peered in. A rumpled bed, pyjamas on the floor, a pair of wellingtons in a corner; on the dressing-table a few masculine toilet articles, hairbrushes, electric shaver and so on.

Evidently Mr. Eldridge was not ill, not here anyway. Just incredibly untidy. She was quietly closing the bedroom door when an angry voice behind her demanded to know what she thought she was doing.

'Who are you?' he asked in Spanish. 'What do you mean by coming in here and——'

'Please forgive me,' she interrupted him in English. 'I made a mistake.'

He stood there menacingly, a tall, broad-shouldered figure in a thick grey sweater, dark brown mud-stained trousers

15

and rubber ankle-boots. His face, which she would judge to be short of handsome at the best of times, was now twisted in a dark scowl. 'Then if you're looking for one of the villas, it isn't this one.'

'I am now quite aware of that,' she said coldly. 'If you'd only give me a few seconds to explain.'

He stood there with folded arms, a smouldering, surly expression on his face. 'I'm waiting, but make it snappy. I haven't time to waste, especially this morning.'

His attitude almost undermined her confidence and had the circumstances been different, she would have fled, but she knew that she had to stand her ground, for this was obviously the permanent tenant, Mr. Eldridge, and she must not antagonise him too much.

'My name is Caran Ingram,' she began in a quiet, controlled voice, 'and I——'

'Caran?' he echoed. 'What sort of name is that?'

She met his glance squarely. 'If you don't like my name, I'm afraid you'll have to put up with it,' she retorted. She was not going into explanations with this arrogant brute. 'If you'll allow me to continue, I've been sent by Mrs. Parmenter, who owns these villas, and I'm staying here for——'

'I hope you'll enjoy yourself, then,' he interrupted. 'This isn't exactly the best time of year for a holiday in these parts, and as for the villas——'

She interrupted him now, her head thrown back, her hazel eyes blazing. 'If you could please listen without interrupting me, you wouldn't jump to the wrong conclusions. I'm not here on holiday. I'm employed by Mrs. Parmenter to manage the villas and see they are properly run.'

'You!' He managed to infuse a world of contempt into that one word. His scornful glance surveyed her from top to toe, taking in her cloudy auburn hair, her usually pale, oval face now pink with indignation, her cream two-piece travelling outfit and her white shoes, now mud-splashed by this morning's walk. 'I don't believe it,' he continued quietly. 'I can't believe that even an English absentee landlord, or rather landlady, would be such a fool as to send someone like you to take on this sort of job.'

'You know nothing about me or what I'm capable of, Mr. Eldridge!' she blazed at him.

'I'm beginning to guess.' The faint hint of a smile lurked around his mouth.

'If you'll kindly tell me which of the villas is the Joyosa, I'll be glad to go there immediately. I was evidently misinformed. I was told that the first villa I came to from the road was the Joyosa. I'm sorry I intruded.' She spoke in sharp staccato sentences, hoping Mr. Eldridge would perceive, if he were capable, her resentment.

'You must have come in from the town end, down that rough and muddy path. The Joyosa is actually the first villa if you approach from the roadway.'

She marched towards the outer door and picked up one of her suitcases, but he took it from her hand. 'I'll bring these and show you where the Villa Joyosa is.'

He did not speak again until he deposited her luggage in the porch of the villa which was to be hers.

'Thank you, Mr. Eldridge,' she said icily.

He pointed to a wooden nameplate over the door. 'This one has its name, as you see. I hope it turns out joyously for you, Miss—what was it?—Ingram, but I must warn you that you can manage all the rest of the villas and their occupants as much as you like if they'll stand for it, but you must leave me alone. I'll stand no interference from anyone. That was understood when I took the place. No spying or prying at all.'

'I've already apologised, and it can hardly be said that I was either spying or prying.'

'Then perhaps you're accustomed to peering into other people's bedrooms?'

'I thought you might be ill.'

'And you see I'm not. Well, I'll be off and leave you to your manager's job for as long as you'll stick it.'

He turned swiftly and stomped off through the gardens.

A totally impossible man, she thought stormily. It was a pity she had accidentally started off on the wrong foot with him, but as he was the only permanent tenant, she need not bother about him, especially as he was so determined to be left alone.

At the moment Caran had other and more urgent problems to solve, for now she was at the door of the Villa Joyosa, her new home, and no keys. She walked around the outside of the villa, but every window was firmly shuttered and a back door was also locked.

She regretted now that she had not asked the man Eldridge where exactly was Manuela's house. There was no one else to ask, so Caran must find the place herself. She walked a short distance up the road and found several small cottages. Outside the first, two small children were playing, but when Caran approached, they ran indoors. The door of the next cottage stood open and Caran banged loudly on the wood, only to be greeted by an impatient shout of *'Qué desea?'* Caran replied that she was looking for Señora Manuela and almost at once an old woman in a rusty black dress came to the door.

She was very small and Caran towered over her. 'I am the English *señorita*, Miss Ingram,' she explained. 'You have the keys of the villas.'

'Sí, sí, señorita.' Manuela trotted inside the cottage and in a moment came out with a bunch of assorted keys, most of them ludicrously large as though they were to open the massive gates of a castle.

'You'd better come with me,' Caran invited. 'I shall need to know what I can about the villas.'

At first Manuela hesitated, then declared that she had the midday meal to cook.

'But these keys aren't labelled,' Caran pointed out. 'How shall I know which fit the doors?'

With a quick gesture, Manuela slammed her front door, which immediately shot open again. 'I come,' she said testily.

'Did you come down to the villas last night?' Caran asked her as they walked down the road.

Manuela paused to stare at the English girl. 'No. Why should I?'

'Oh.' Caran thought it useless to pursue that subject further or go into explanations of how she had spent the night in the town. All the same, Mrs. Parmenter's manage-

18

ment seemed to be extremely lacking in efficiency.

By now the pair had arrived at the Villa Joyosa and Manuela sorted out one of the bunch of keys and tried it in the lock. But evidently it was not the correct one, and she tried two others, of which the second fitted. The interior was dark with the shuttered windows and the whole place smelt musty, but Caran could attend to all these things afterwards. Her intuition warned her that on this first inspection of the villas she must have a witness to accompany her. After the unfortunate incident of Mr. Eldridge, Caran was anxious to be careful.

The next villa, Turquesa, was also shuttered, but when she and Manuela came to the third, called Cristal, the front door was open. 'Is someone living here?' she asked the old woman. 'I understood that all except one were empty.'

'No, there is no one there,' declared Manuela, 'but you have the key.'

She took Caran's wrist as though to guide her away, but at that moment a woman's voice began a snatch of song and three small children came running out of the villa, only to pause and eye Caran shyly, but then they ran towards Manuela, tugging at her dress or grabbing one of her hands.

'I'd better see who occupies this villa,' Caran said decisively. Manuela, with the children still clinging to her skirts, tried ineffectually to prevent Caran from entering, but Caran was not to be hindered. She walked quickly through the living room into the kitchen. A young woman was washing clothes in the sink and when she saw Caran she broke off her song in mid-syllable, put her wet hands to her mouth, then screamed piercingly at the sight of Manuela.

'What goes on?' demanded Caran. 'Who are you and why are you living here?'

Between the hysterical sobbing of the younger woman and the shrill explanations of Manuela, Caran gathered the story. This was Manuela's elder daughter, Gabriela, who with her husband and five children, had been turned out of the cottage where they had lived because they could not pay the rent.

'So Gabriela brought the children here,' explained Manuela. 'Only for a week or two until her husband finds another place.'

'But that was quite wrong,' declared Caran. 'These villas are private and should not be used like that.'

'Why not?' demanded the old woman. 'They are empty in winter. In summer rich people come to live here. Why must we not put a roof over the children?'

Caran was aware of a certain sympathy with the local people who would obviously be tempted to occupy an empty villa where there was no supervision. Besides, Manuela held the keys.

The daughter, Gabriela, maintained that she had looked after the villa well and kept it clean. She had done no damage.

Caran said that she would consider the matter, but Gabriela and her husband must speedily find somewhere else to live.

What would she find in the next villa? she wondered. But the one named Esmeralda had no occupants other than a few spiders. Manuela refused to conduct Caran to the last villa, Zafiro.

'Is it occupied by another family?' Caran queried, half amused by the old woman's reluctance.

'No, no, *señorita*, but a man is living there. He does not like visitors. He does not let me have the key.'

Caran smiled. 'I've already met him—Señor Eldridge. Yes, we will leave him alone today.' Caran had no desire to meet that man a second time today. She took all the keys from Manuela. 'I shall need some help, Manuela, in cleaning out the Villa Joyosa today. Can you ask your daughter?'

'Not that one. My young daughter, Benita, will come,' Manuela promised. 'This afternoon.'

Before Caran could ask any further questions or get more information, Manuela had scuttled away down the path that led towards the road where she lived.

Caran gave a deep sigh. No wonder Mrs. Parmenter had decided to engage someone to live on the spot to look after her five villas!

'They must all be repainted and repaired,' she had told

Caran, 'and the work must be completed by the end of January or sooner. The tourist agents send their inspectors then and I lost a lot of bookings earlier this year because they said my villas were below standard for letting.'

The estimates and arrangements for the redecorating had all been made, Mrs. Parmenter continued, so all Caran had to do was set things in motion.

Caran now walked thoughtfully towards her own villa, the Joyosa. There was certainly an irony about the name. How much joy was she going to extract from this already discouraging situation? The villas themselves would revive if they were cleaned and painted, the gardens needed clearing and tidying, but how was she to evict Gabriela and her family? As to the detestable Mr. Eldridge, she would leave him severely alone.

She was beginning to see the meaning of those wary glances and abrupt changes of subject when she had mentioned the villas to Don Ramiro and then to Señora Molina. Was it only because the whole cluster was ill-kept? Or was there some other reason?

Caran dumped her suitcases inside, but before unpacking them her first task was to open the shutters and windows of the villa and let in some fresh air and light. She made a brief tour of the rooms. Once it was all cleaned, the living room would be attractive, she thought, with its whitewashed walls, now grimy and with cobwebbed corners. The floor of olive green and white marble was dusty and stained, but needed only a thorough scrubbing. The furnishings were sparse, just a table of black wood and three or four chairs with cushioned seats. A long, low chest stood at one end and Caran, peering inside, found that the last occupants had left a fine assortment of empty wine bottles behind them.

In the bedroom she was dismayed to find that a bedspread seemed to have been thrown over the mattress, for there were no pillows, sheets or blankets. Perhaps all the linen was in a cupboard somewhere, but her search revealed none.

The kitchen was small, but probably adequate for holiday use in a villa intended for only two people. Some of the other villas were much larger, accommodating up to six persons.

With a start, it occurred to her that there was only one single bed in the bedroom. Where was the other? Mrs. Parmenter had given her a fairly rough inventory of the contents of the various villas and Caran decided to refer to it as soon as possible.

By midday she had cleaned out a chest of drawers and a wardrobe and stowed away her clothes and possessions, but there was no sign of the girl who was coming to clean the place.

She went along to the villa occupied by Gabriela and her family and asked when she might expect Benita.

'My mother told you Benita would come?' queried Gabriela. 'But she works in the town.'

'Who? Benita? Then when was she supposed to be coming?' demanded Caran.

Gabriela shrugged her plump shoulders. 'Perhaps tonight after the shop is shut.'

Caran was aware that Continental shops keep open much later than English ones. In any case it would be dark by about five o'clock and she had not yet discovered what lighting there might be.

'Well, I must have the rooms cleaned properly today,' she said firmly.

Gabriela's dark eyes held an expression of anxiety compounded with fear. Then she turned to what seemed to be the eldest of her brood and gave the child instructions to go up to the cottage where Manuela lived and tell Benita to come as soon as she came home for the midday meal.

'I will also come,' promised Gabriela. 'You have no hot water.'

'Oh? Then you must tell me how to make the arrangements for hot water and the cooking and so on. Also, there is no bed linen.'

Gabriela told her that all the spare linen was stored in the Villa Esmeralda, the largest of the five, where the cupboards were more capacious.

'And what has happened to the second bed in my villa?' Caran wanted to know.

Gabriela bowed her head and did not answer.

'Come, Gabriela, where is it? I must know.' By now Caran had a shrewd idea of exactly where the bed was.

'I—we—borrowed it,' Gabriela admitted after a pause. 'The children, you see. There were not enough beds here for all of us.'

Caran began to wonder how much other furniture had been 'borrowed' from the various villas by Gabriela and her family. 'We'll talk about that later,' she said. 'In the meantime, please send your sister to my villa as soon as she can come.'

Walking back through the gardens, Caran now saw that the layout of the villas was excellent. Although they were all connected by a common path running parallel with the sea-shore, each villa had its own individual approach and was secluded in its own part of the gardens. It occurred to her that this morning she had been so busy trying to settle in that she had not even glanced at the surroundings. Magnolia trees and oleanders, orange and lemon trees had been planted and now provided adequate screens to the villas. At this time of year there was not the blaze of colour that would appear in a couple of months' time, but there were a number of shrubs and bushes with bright orange flowers or scarlet berries, and the dark purple bougainvillea trailed over every available support.

Beyond the main path lay a sloping strip of rough, stony land dipping to the pale golden beach below and the shimmering aquamarine sea. To the left was a small peninsula jutting out and Caran climbed to the top of a ridge so that she could see the other side. There was no beach beyond the spit of land, for the sea lapped the edge of the rocky shore.

In the opposite direction she had a view of almost the whole of the town of Albarosa, its square, white, Moorish houses climbing tier on tier up the rocky hillside. As soon as she had put her own villa reasonably straight she would take the first opportunity of exploring this unusual-looking town.

By the time Caran returned to the Villa Joyosa, Benita and Gabriela were already busy cleaning and scrubbing, shaking rugs and generally giving the place a good turn-out.

Benita was a good deal younger than her sister, not more

23

than seventeen or eighteen, Caran judged. A pretty girl with liquid brown eyes, black hair that curled around her shoulders, a full rich mouth that frequently curved happily into smiles.

Caran enquired about the hot water system and some form of heating, for at this time of year the nights would be chilly even if the daytime warmth was acceptable.

Benita showed her how to manipulate the gas cooker and water heater. There was a small gas fire in the living room, Caran was glad to know. Electricity was used only for lighting, but when Benita switched on, only one bulb out of the four in the lighting fitment came to life. The other lamps had probably gone into Gabriela's villa, thought Caran grimly.

With many smiles and cheerful remarks, the two sisters assured Caran that everything would be clean and orderly in a couple of hours. *'Nuevecito'*, they said, and Caran enjoyed a hilarious few moments in translating the word into its English equivalent of 'spick and span'. 'Speak y spahn,' muttered Benita many times over, no doubt memorising the phrase to work off on some unsuspecting and mystified companion.

Caran realised that she was very hungry indeed, but she hesitated to say so or the girls would offer her something to eat straightaway. Instead, she said casually, 'I should like to see part of the town. Which is the best way?'

Benita gave her directions up the winding road into Albarosa, the way she should have come down this morning.

'And perhaps there is a restaurant or café where I can eat?'

'Yes, the one called El Catalan,' Gabriela suggested. 'You will find it easily, for it's in the main square. There are also others, but not so good.'

Caran changed her shoes, slipped a white wool jacket over her tangerine tricel dress and set off. She carefully tucked all her money and travellers' cheques into her handbag, for she did not yet know how much she could trust Gabriela and Benita, although as they were Spanish, they were probably extremely honest.

The October sun showed her a very different Albarosa from the glimpses she had seen of the town last night in the pouring rain and this morning she had been too intent on following the man Vicente to spare time to notice the buildings. But now she had the opportunity to approach the rising town, its square, white, flat-roofed houses crowning the rocky hill and seeming to tumble down the slopes like a child's box of bricks carelessly scattered.

Mauve hills and a deep blue sky made a perfect backcloth of this dazzling little town. The distance along the road was farther than she had imagined and she realised now that Vicente had conducted her the shortest, if rougher, way.

Once in the town now she was delighted with everything she saw. Busy squares, dark little alleyways that led through arches to streets where oranges, grapes and figs were sold from stalls or barrows. Sometimes she walked along streets where on one side houses of three or four storeys reared above her head and on the other, she was on roof top level. There were innumerable flights of steps between tall, narrow houses and, having thoroughly lost herself, except for a sense of the slope of the town, she was relieved to find herself again in a square where tables were set outside the cafés, but in an arcade with Moorish arches.

She looked for El Catalan and found it in a corner. Tubs and boxes of flowers adorned the front and she sat down at a table in the sun.

She decided to eat a leisurely meal, for there was no hurry to return to her villa and no doubt soon she would have little leisure to dawdle about the town. She ordered a glass of wine and the inevitable *tapas*, tiny saucers of savoury tit-bits, small fish or morsels of smoked mountain ham. A dish of *paella* followed by fruit and cheese completed the meal, and she was surprised by the modest bill.

She spent the rest of the afternoon browsing among the shops. Mrs. Parmenter had told her that Albarosa was so far completely unspoilt and as far as souvenir shops and other tourist traps were concerned, Caran could see for herself that this was so. Also, there were several small inns or restaurants that offered accommodation, but she had not yet seen anything in the nature of a large hotel.

So there was probably not much choice for Don Ramiro last night except to deposit her with his friend, Señora Molina. Caran wondered if she would ever meet the tall, handsome Spaniard again, but as his home was in Almeria there was little likelihood of that.

It occurred to her that she must obviously provide herself with a small amount of food for the next day or so. After that, she would be able to make arrangements for supplies to be delivered to her. She made her purchases and then sat for half an hour outside a café where she could drink coffee and watch the passers-by.

Tomorrow she would have to get down to serious work, study all the instructions and documents Mrs. Parmenter had given her and tackle all the people who were to work on the decorations and re-painting. Today she could surely afford to idle.

Lights appeared in shop windows and in the café behind her and she suddenly realised that she might have wasted too much time. Darkness would overtake her before she could reach the villas. She gathered her parcels and handbag, left payment for the coffee and hurried off out of the square, but she mistook her direction, for soon she found herself in a steep street that was unlit except for the glimmer of white houses on either side. A beam of light shone from a doorway and she paused, uncertain whether to ask for direction. Two men came out and she saw their figures silhouetted against the light.

It was ridiculous to be frightened, she told herself, yet she was aware that in her handbag she was carrying all her present available wealth. She hung back in the shadows until the two men disappeared.

If only she had some hope of finding a taxi, but there was little chance of that. Presently she came to a better-lighted corner and here she asked an elderly woman to direct her to the main square.

As she had begun to suspect, Caran had to retrace the way she had come. Somewhere she had taken a wrong turn and she was now descending the hill on the far side of the town away from the villas.

In the darkness it was difficult to avoid stumbling over large stones, for the road was not paved, but eventually she was in a more populated part and this time she asked again for the Plaza.

She was so thankful to reach the centre of the town that she decided to rest before setting out again. It was still early evening although completely dark, and she could not now reach the Villa Joyosa in even a semblance of daylight.

After an omelette in a nearby café, she asked the waiter for precise instructions, but he was uncertain and consulted a colleague. Caran sketched the streets and turnings on the back of an envelope and the two waiters assured her that this time she could not possibly make a mistake.

More than half an hour later, Caran was grimly assuring herself that she was capable of any amount of mistakes, for the path had become so rough she was convinced she had missed the top road and was now descending that same path she had trodden this morning with Vicente.

Oh, well, sooner or later she'd arrive, she told herself, and preferably in one piece. Several times she stumbled and once fell full length on the slightly raised bank at the side of the path. Her eyes had become accustomed to the total darkness and she could just pick out the slightly less dark strip of boulder-strewn earth. A pity she had left the road, which would have been a longer, but probably much safer route.

Suddenly she became aware of someone approaching and the next instant a torch was shining full in her eyes.

As she gasped with fright, an English voice exclaimed, 'Well, of all the miracles! If it isn't our very own lady manageress!'

'Oh, you must be Mr. Eldridge.' Relief that he was at least a person she had already met could not be disguised in her tone of voice, but she was resentfully aware of his unnecessarily sarcastic manner.

'What do you think you're doing scrambling down here at this time of night?' he demanded. 'Trying to break your neck?'

'It's not late,' she retorted.

'Too late for tenderfoots like you. Even I have the sense to bring a torch with me, and I know the ups and downs of the ground pretty thoroughly.'

'It wasn't really dark when I first started for home,' she explained, 'but I lost my way and went in the wrong direction.'

'I could have guessed that,' he replied curtly. 'Well, I'll have to take you to the villas, I suppose.'

'Thank you, Mr. Eldridge,' she said icily, 'but having come this far and managed not to break my neck, I expect I can cope with the rest of the way.' They were brave words and at the instant she spoke she was determined not to expect his help.

'Don't be daft! The end of the path is worse than this.'

He took her arm and marched her a few steps along the track. Then he apparently realised that she had several parcels and he took a couple out of her hand.

He led her past his own villa, along the lower path and eventually to the Villa Joyosa. Neither had exchanged a word, but when she stood in the arched entrance porch of the villa, she said quietly, 'Thank you, Mr. Eldridge. I realise that I ought not to have tackled that path in the dark until I know it better.'

'I should think not!' he snapped. 'If I hadn't met you on my way up to the town for dinner, who knows what might have happened? We might even have lost our new manageress, lying helpless all night and not discovered until tomorrow morning. You could have died of exposure.'

She could have slapped his face, but restrained herself. At least he had conducted her home in safety.

'I'm sorry I've delayed you having your dinner.'

'I can wait. What sort of shape is your villa in?'

She was surprised at his curiosity. 'I don't really know yet,' she admitted. 'Those two sisters, Gabriela and Benita, were supposed to clean the place and I left them to it.'

He touched a switch in the porch and lights came on from a swinging lamp and another fitment in the hall.

'Oh, I hadn't known about those lights,' she said.

'You've a whole lot to learn, haven't you?'

In the amber light from the porch, she glanced at his face, seeing the angular planes of his features, his dark, reddish hair, but the expression in his eyes she could not see.

'Go on in,' he suggested. 'At least I can probably show you where the light switches are. Besides, I'd like to inspect the place so that I can see where my own deficiencies lie. I'm sure your brief inspection of my villa must have shocked you with my untidiness.'

'If you insist on coming in, I suppose I can't stop you.'

There was nothing for it but to unlock the door and let him follow. He was one of Mrs. Parmenter's tenants and she had to make the best of that situation, but she hoped with all her heart that she would not have to meet him frequently. He had already commanded her this morning to leave him alone and this she would do with supreme pleasure.

CHAPTER TWO

GABRIELA and her sister had certainly accomplished a considerable change in the appearance of the Villa Joyosa. The living room, revealed now in all its full complement of four light bulbs, was spotless, the furniture polished, the rugs neatly in place on the washed marble floor. The litter of empty wine bottles had been cleared from the chest and on top stood a tray with glasses, a bottle of local wine and a corkscrew. Beside it was an ornamental dish of oranges and figs.

'Oh, isn't that charming!' Caran exclaimed.

'Just an old Spanish custom,' murmured Mr. Eldridge behind her. 'A glass of wine is intended to bring good luck to a new occupant.'

He followed her to the kitchen where again everything seemed to be in order. Then she stepped along the passage to the bedroom. Still only one bed, but that was properly made and the coverlet neatly turned down.

When she returned to the living room Mr. Eldridge was tossing the corkscrew in his hand. 'Shall I open this for you?' He indicated the bottle of wine.

Really, the man was quite unpredictable! One minute he was ordering her to keep off the grass, the next he was insinuating himself into her life before she had properly taken up residence here in the villa.

'Thank you,' she answered politely. 'Perhaps you will join me in drinking to the success of this new occupant. In any case, one can't drink alone.'

As the cork came out with a satisfactory plop, he raised his head and glanced at her face. 'Not overloaded with tact, are you?' was his comment. 'You'll have to do better than that when the summertime comes and you have these hordes of visitors in and out, complaining about the heat, the service, the maid and everything else they can think of.'

He handed her the glass of pale yellow wine. 'What shall

we drink to?' he asked.

'The Villa Joyosa and its successful tenant,' she replied with a touch of defiance.

'Agreed!' He tossed off the wine and stood there holding the empty glass.

There was something about his stance, his attitude, that indicated his reluctance to leave. Well, she thought, if he were waiting for an invitation to a meal, she was not going to pander to him. Yet the practical side of her cried out that here was an opportunity to find out some of the problems connected with the villas. Mrs. Parmenter had not really prepared Caran for what she would find.

'I've delayed you when you were on your way to dinner,' she began tentatively.

'All right. I'll accept the marching orders.'

He set down his glass carefully on the tray and walked towards the door.

'You wouldn't care to stay and have a meal?' she offered.

He swung round. 'Can I trust your cooking?'

'You'll have to risk it if you wish to stay.'

He grinned at her. 'You'll probably blow yourself up on an unfamiliar cooker if I don't give you a hand. What's on offer?'

'Not very much, I'm afraid.' She went out to the kitchen where the food had been set down. 'Some smoked ham, tomatoes, a couple of tins of pâté, bread rolls. I had a melon, but I seem to have lost that on the way down, probably when I fell over.'

'Just as well you weren't carrying eggs. Or were you?'

'No.' Then they laughed in unison, the first time in harmonious companionship.

'I'll go along to my place and bring back some butter and coffee to start you off,' he offered.

'How do we get supplies here? Is there someone who will deliver orders?'

He twisted his mouth into a wry shape. 'There was, but somehow the bills didn't get paid, so you'll have to start again to build up your credit. I'll be back in ten minutes.'

As Caran set out plates and cutlery she reflected on the

31

strangeness of this man. She understood why he insisted on his own privacy, especially to an English girl. He would not want a compatriot walking into his villa just when she chose. This morning—could it be only the morning of this same day?—he had brusquely told her to get out. Tonight he had practically invited himself to supper with her.

If he were one of those men who cautiously peer out of their shell for a time, then, afraid of their rashness, dodge back in case some undesirable experience happens to them, then Caran knew she would have to make the most of this single evening. It was in any case an unexpected encounter, for if she had kept to the top road, she would never have met him coming up the short-cut path on his way to the town.

He had not returned in the ten minutes he promised and she smiled. So already he had regretted his imprudence in entering her villa. Probably he was calling himself all kinds of fool.

When half an hour had elapsed, she decided that he was not coming back. She put the food away in the refrigerator, for having eaten fairly recently, she was not hungry.

Then he came stumbling in, laden with bags and boxes of food.

'Did you think I wasn't coming?' he asked.

'Yes.'

'A blunt girl if ever I saw one,' he muttered, setting down in the kitchen the groceries he had brought with him—a box of eggs, a bottle of milk, a jar of coffee, butter and, surprisingly, a string of onions.

'It's very good of you to bring all these,' she said, infusing gratitude into her tone.

'Yes, it is,' he agreed. 'Don't worry, you'll probably be charged up for all the items.' He gave her a crooked smile as he buttered an omelette pan and put it on the gas flame.

The resulting meal proved that Mr. Eldridge was a creditable cook, even if, as he admitted, his range of menus was limited.

'Can you tell me where I'm to get supplies of provisions and so on?' she asked him. 'I know that every visitor must have a stock already in the fridge to start with, and of course, I shall need to eat without traipsing to the town every day for shopping.'

'I'll give you a list of the shops, but first you must go there personally and tell them that you're the new lady manageress of the villas and that you will pay for everything by the month. These villas have a bad name for credit.'

'Why was that?'

'The agents who were supposed to be responsible didn't give the right instructions or send the money.'

'Was it a Spanish company?'

'No. English. A Spanish concern might be at fault in some respects, but they wouldn't defraud their own shopkeepers.'

'I understood from Mrs. Parmenter, the owner, that she'd tried both English and Spanish agents to look after the villas and neither had been successful.'

He cut himself a hunk of cheese. 'What did she expect? She buys a few villas, lets them to tourists and is convinced that she's going to make a fortune.'

'She needs the income,' Caran pointed out. 'She's put her capital into the villas as an investment and expects it to pay the right dividends.'

'So the whole place would pay and pay handsomely, if only it were properly run.'

'That's why I'm here,' she reminded him. 'Mrs. Parmenter said she was tired of losing early lettings because the villas weren't up to standard.'

'But her trouble is that when she loses lettings, she tries to make up the loss by much higher prices for the summer visitors. People are probably willing to pay, but they expect a certain service in return. This last summer, for instance, there was not enough maids. Benita could look after only two villas at a time, although she tried to do more.'

'Where were the other maids, then?'

'Just not engaged. Plenty of girls in the town would be willing to come if the wages and conditions were right, but they're not going to slave for nothing.'

'Was Benita supposed to clean and look after the villas all through the winter?' she asked.

'I suppose so, but you can't blame the girl if she finds that

33

there's no supervision, all the villas empty except mine, and gets herself a job in the town. It's quite likely that her wages weren't paid.'

Caran was thoughtful. 'I seem to have a formidable task before me,' she murmured.

'You certainly have. How much did you find out about all this lot before you took on the job?'

She smiled wryly. 'Not enough, evidently. But I shall make these villas so popular and well run that there'll be a waiting list.'

His oblique glance conveyed his scepticism.

'Mrs. Parmenter has two new ones being built. I haven't seen them yet,' Caran continued.

'Only half finished. They're on the other side of the little neck of land that sticks out in a point. You'll have to chase up the builders if you want those two finished in time for next summer.'

'How long have Gabriela and her family been occupying one of the villas?' was her next question.

He considered for a moment. 'About six weeks or so.'

'How on earth am I going to get them out? Her mother said the family had been turned out of where they were living.'

'Yes, so I heard. They couldn't pay the rent.'

'Well, they'll simply have to go. Otherwise we shall have other families taking possession of empty villas.'

'Exactly,' he agreed. 'You mustn't be too soft.'

'What does Gabriela's husband do for a living?' she asked after a pause.

'He's a waiter at a restaurant in the town, El Catalan.'

'Oh, I see. Gabriela recommended me to go there today for a meal.'

'It's not bad,' Mr. Eldridge conceded. 'He doesn't earn much, of course, but at least he's able to bring some food home with him. Otherwise they'd all starve.'

Caran's heart was filled with pity for this unfortunate family and could sympathise with Gabriela's temptation to occupy, even for a few weeks, an empty villa.

'M'm,' she said now. 'I shall have to see what I can do to

34

find them other accommodation.'

'Have you influence with the local authorities, d'you think?' His tone was unmistakably sardonic.

'None, of course, but I was thinking that I know someone who might be most influential. His name is Señor Mendosa.'

'Don Ramiro?' he echoed. 'That Mendosa?'

When she nodded, he continued, 'How on earth do you know Don Ramiro?'

She explained a trifle huffily that Don Ramiro had driven her from Granada airport, found her a lodging for the night at the house of one of his friends, Señora Molina.

'You mean you arrived at the airport without any definitely arranged transport? Why didn't you stay the night in Granada?'

'That was my intention until I was told that someone going my way would give me a lift.'

He snorted with amusement. 'Aren't you the greenest girl?' he said when at last he could speak. 'If you allow yourself to be picked up at night for a long car ride by any handsome Spaniard, you're heading for trouble, my girl.'

'Don Ramiro was very kind and I was grateful for his help,' she said stiffly.

'I'll bet he'd already spotted you in the airport and hoped you were going his way.'

'Since he apparently lives in Almeria, he came considerably out of his way to bring me to Albarosa last night.'

'Oh, certainly he has a house in Almeria, but he has several others besides, including a villa here in Albarosa.'

'I didn't know that.'

'I don't suppose he'd tell you that. He'd prefer to pose as the perfect Spanish gentleman, the nobleman with the purest of motives.'

'You seem to dislike him,' she observed drily.

'Even your opinion may possibly change when you know him better.'

'It's doubtful whether I shall ever meet him again.'

'You sound wistful,' he told her. 'If you're anxious to know him better, I can no doubt arrange a meeting for you.'

'Please don't bother on my behalf,' she said hastily. 'I only mentioned his name in passing, as it were.'

He gave a long, exaggerated sigh. 'Let's talk of something else. Tell me why you've taken on this ridiculous job.'

'Ridiculous? Why?'

'It's completely ridiculous at your age.'

'I'm nearly twenty-two,' she protested. 'Some people manage to credit me with a little sense.'

'Sense is not enough. You can't work here by the same commonsense standards you'd use in England. The people are different. Proud and stubborn, they prefer to be coaxed rather than driven.'

She told him why she had taken the post Mrs. Parmenter had offered.

'And your family? Don't they mind?' he queried.

'They trust me to behave reasonably.'

'And not put yourself into the clutches of handsome Dons.'

She smouldered at his goading tone, but refused to answer. She wondered what sort of job kept him here in Spain, but she would not dream of asking him.

He finished his coffee and rose to go. 'I must be off. I've work to do.'

'Then I'll not keep you. Thank you for bringing so much food and drink.'

She walked with him towards the front porch.

'*Buenas noches,*' he said. 'Sleep well.'

'Good night, Mr. Eldridge.'

'My name is Brooke Eldridge,' he informed her. 'I'd better tell you, because sometimes there's confusion when parcels or messages arrive addressed to Señor Brooke.'

'I shan't take advantage and start calling you by your Christian name,' she assured him. 'Good night, Mr. Eldridge.'

In the light of the porch lantern she saw his momentary check, his eyelids lowered. Then he went through the arch. 'Don't dream too much of the handsome Don Ramiro,' was his parting injunction.

'Dreams usually come unbidden!' she called out, but he had already disappeared into the darkness.

Returning to the living room and clearing away the remains of the supper, she reflected that today had indeed been a remarkable initiation into the formidable task that lay ahead.

She could not decide at this stage of their acquaintance whether Mr. Brooke Eldridge intended to be friendly and co-operative or whether he would refuse to fall in with any plans that did not suit him.

He had not disclosed what his job was and she was curious as to what sort of work could claim him at this time of night, nearly half-past ten. Perhaps he was studying for some profession and needed as much solitude as possible.

She set her alarm clock for seven next morning and fell into a dreamless sleep, unpopulated by any handsome Spaniards or even acid-tongued Englishmen.

The water for her morning shower was stone cold and she realised that she had forgotten to set the time switch last night. She made a note of her omission, for this was one of the small annoyances that upset visitors at the start. They must be told exactly what was to be done.

She realised now what a difference it might make to the smooth running of the villas to have someone like herself in the initial position of a visitor. Caran was the guinea-pig who would have to discover all the flaws and put them right.

After breakfast, her first task was to arrange for supplies of provisions to be sent down to her villa and she went along to the Villa Cristal to ask Gabriela for information.

Gabriela was, as usual, washing children's clothes and immediately appeared apprehensive when Caran called.

'You have come to turn us out?' she queried.

'Not yet,' replied Caran, 'but of course, something must be done in the next few days.'

Gabriela wrung her wet hands in anxiety. 'We have nowhere to go, no place to live,' she said tremulously.

'Well, forget that for the moment. I want your help.'

Caran explained in her careful Spanish that she wanted the names of reliable food shops in Albarosa. It would have been better to rely more on Brooke Eldridge's promised list, but she could not disturb him this morning and allow him to imagine that she was running after him for every little detail as soon as she had arrived.

Gabriela offered the information that her sister, Benita, worked in a fairly large grocers' that sold delicatessen and wines. Caran thought this might do for a start for her own supplies. Later, she would contact other shops in case they were more competitive.

Benita was serving in the shop when Caran called and placed her order.

'Thank you and your sister for cleaning and tidying my villa so well yesterday,' she said, as she chose butter and ham. 'Also for the bottle of wine. That was thoughtful of you. Put it down on the bill.'

The girl wrote down the order and offered numerous extra items which Caran might like to try.

'That's enough for the time being,' decided Caran. 'Will you deliver today? Villa Joyosa.'

A middle-aged man, swarthy, with a small black moustache, emerged from behind a stand of wine bottles.

'Villa Joyosa?' he queried, then shook his head. 'The money first.'

Caran made no bones about this brusque demand, for she realised, as Brooke Eldridge had pointed out, that she must build up credit and a good name for the villas all over again.

She handed him the amount and waited for a receipt. As Caran was leaving, Benita whispered, 'You should have had the order sent to Señor Eldridge. He does not pay first.'

Caran smiled. *'No importa.'* At this stage it did not matter whether she had to pay for everything in advance, but later on the bills would be settled regularly as they came in.

Near a fountain in a small square she bought flowers from an old woman surrounded by brilliant splashes of colour. Lilies, mimosa, poinsettias and some spiky blue flowers which the flower-seller called *'lanzas'*. Caran agreed that they looked like beautiful lances or spears and the botanical name would probably not describe them half so well. She chose an assorted bunch and set out for the house of Señora Molina.

The *señora* was delighted with the flowers. *'Esplendido!'*

38

she exclaimed.

'It's the only way I can thank you for your kindness and hospitality of two nights ago,' said Caran.

Señora Molina shrugged. 'It was nothing. I was glad to help you and also to do something for Don Ramiro.'

'I was sorry to bring him so far out of his way. Perhaps when you see him again, you will tell him how grateful I was for his assistance.'

Señora Molina gave Caran a long, level look. Then she nodded. 'I will get you a glass of wine.' As she handed Caran the glass, she said, 'You are young to take this work with the villas.'

'Oh, I shall manage,' Caran answered lightly.

'Everything goes well?'

Caran frowned slightly. 'Not exactly, but then I've barely had time to straighten things out.'

After she left Señora Molina, Caran spent an hour in the town centre, trying to learn its geography so that she should not be lost a second time.

During the afternoon she visited the site of the two new villas and inspected progress. Half finished, Brooke Eldridge had declared. As far as she could see, there was still more than half the work to be done on them, for the walls were only partly built, building materials lay in uncovered heaps and the site had an abandoned air.

She made a few notes, then walked farther down towards the shore. The view from here was undoubtedly magnificent; towards the east a tree-clad headland sloping down to the sea, the small curving bay a deep emerald green. On the other side the long crescent of sandy beach and behind the palms and chestnut trees the villas only partially visible. Mrs. Parmenter had chosen her site well and Caran was now determined to make the little cluster of villas a satisfactory investment for her employer.

For the next two or three days she called on the various firms and workmen concerned with the building of the two new villas and the redecorating of the others. In every case she was greeted with perfect courtesy, but there was a certain lack of enthusiasm. The painters said they were busy with many other orders and the villas must wait. The builders declared that they had no further instructions and could not complete unless they were paid by instalments whenever an amount of work was finished.

Caran perceived that here again reluctance to work on the villas was obviously inspired by lack of confidence in being eventually paid.

'I have authority to pay you as soon as the work is done,' she told them all, and the foreman of the building firm agreed that he would come next day and assess what was to be started.

Other firms expressed anxiety because she was only a young English girl who did not understand the situation. Two firms showed her unpaid bills outstanding from the early part of the summer. If these were paid soon, they would consider doing further work.

She wrote down particulars of all her calls and visits and one afternoon she worked on a long report for Mrs. Parmenter. She asked for the transfer of more money so that she could pay the outstanding bills and have something in hand for the most urgent jobs. Of Gabriela and her family occupying one of the villas she said nothing yet, for she hoped to be able to get them out within a short time.

A shadow fell across the page she was typing. 'Don Ramiro!' She rose hastily from the little table where she had set her portable typewriter in the wide porch of the villa. 'I wasn't expecting you.'

'I hope I am not unwelcome, for I see you are very busy,' he said.

'I'd practically finished,' she told him. 'Will you come in?'

'I think I prefer to sit here.' He pulled forward one of the wicker chairs from the corner of the porch.

'Then may I offer you coffee or a glass of wine?'

'Not yet. I came to see if you were settled here. Does everything go smoothly?'

Caran grimaced. 'I'm afraid it doesn't. I'm finding all sorts of unexpected problems and troubles, but I'm sure I shall get them solved within a week or so.'

'What sort of troubles?' he queried.

'There has been much bad management in the past and this makes it difficult to get things done now.' She related her experiences with the various builders and painters.

He was sympathetic. 'Would you care to let me see the villas?'

She agreed instantly. A word or two from Don Ramiro in the right direction might work wonders, she reflected, for he was probably well known in Albarosa.

When they approached the Villa Cristal, two of Gabriela's smaller children were playing in front of the porch.

'This one is already let?' Don Ramiro asked.

'No.' Caran was forced to explain. 'It's occupied by a family who have apparently been turned out of their former house.'

'And they can pay the rent of such a villa?' he queried.

She flushed. 'At present they're not paying anything. They're very poor indeed. That's why they lost their other place, I believe. They couldn't pay the rent.'

'I should like to meet this woman,' he said in a tone of authority.

The two children scuttled away like lizards as Caran and Don Ramiro approached, and evidently their excited cries and shouts brought Gabriela out of her kitchen.

At the sight of this tall man accompanying Caran, Gabriela almost cringed with terror.

'This is Gabriela,' murmured Caran, smiling at the woman. 'I don't know her surname.'

'Gabriela Ribera,' she supplied without being asked. Then she began to gabble incoherently in Spanish, begging Don Ramiro not to throw her and her children into the street.

'My husband is a good man. Felipe works hard and does his best, but he doesn't earn much money.' She put her hands over her face and sobbed heartrendingly.

Don Ramiro listened in silence.

Seeing their mother in distress, the two children clung to her and added their crying to hers.

Caran said gently, 'Gabriela, we have not come to turn you out. Don Ramiro is a friend.'

The woman raised her tear-stained face. 'Friend! Then you will help us? We do not want to stay here, because we know it is forbidden, but a small place that we could afford, oh, we would be so happy!'

She touched Don Ramiro's arm and Caran noticed how he drew away.

'I can promise nothing,' he said at last. 'But you must find somewhere else to go.' He turned away and walked down the path. Caran knew she must follow, but she whispered hurriedly, 'Don't worry, Gabriela. We'll find something for you.'

When she caught up with Don Ramiro, who had waited for her on the lower path, she murmured, 'Poor woman! She doesn't know where to turn.'

'You must not let sympathy and pity influence you too much,' he cautioned her. 'In our country, as in every country, there are careless people who do not know how to live or pay their debts. Then they expect others to come to their rescue.'

Caran sighed. 'Oh, I know I shall have to get them out. They should never have been allowed in, but Gabriela's mother had charge of the keys, so it was perhaps only natural that she should let her daughter take one of the villas.'

Don Ramiro did not reply and Caran assumed that he was annoyed because he had been involved in a distressing scene. At the Villa Esmeralda, the last but one, he rubbed his hand along some of the outside plaster and when it flaked off, he remarked, 'These are not well built. The workmanship is poor.'

Caran bridled. 'They may not be as well constructed as one would prefer, but they are mainly for summer use,' she pointed out.

'And in the winter they are neglected and show their faults.'

'I shall be here to look after them, winter or summer,' she declared.

At that he glanced at her and smiled. 'You sound as

though you have adopted your task for many years to come.'

'How do you know that I might not want to stay here permanently? I might like this part of Spain so much that I couldn't bear to leave it.'

'Oh, Spain, yes. My country appeals to the heart. People believe that they come and go as they please. They do not realise that Spain has wound slender chains around them and when they stray too far, the chain is tugged and they come back.'

A poetic way of putting it, Caran thought, but she granted that all Don Ramiro said might be true.

By now they had left the Villa Esmeralda and Caran hesitated. 'There is one more, the Villa Zafiro,' she explained, 'but that is permanently occupied.'

'By someone who really pays the rent?'

'Oh, yes. He's English and he works here, I believe. His name is Eldridge, Brooke Eldridge.'

Don Ramiro turned towards her. 'That is very good that you have one of your own countrymen so near at hand to guide you. I suppose he's the young man who works on the irrigation scheme up in the hills.'

'Oh, is that what he does?' Caran's memory leapt back to that first day when she had poked her nose into Mr. Eldridge's villa. The wellingtons, the thigh-boots, the serviceable jacket, all these pointed to a wet and watery job.

'There are two new villas being built for my employer,' Caran said. 'Would you like to see them? There's not much to see yet, because the building work seems to have stopped suddenly.'

'I know about them,' answered Don Ramiro. 'They are set in a very bad place.'

Caran stared at him. 'A bad place? But why? The views from there are superb.'

Don Ramiro smiled. 'Perhaps that is what I meant. Bad for those who are not fortunate enough to be living in them.'

Caran was puzzled, but since such a tremendous amount of work had to be done before these two were habitable, the point was not worth arguing about.

She and her escort had nearly reached the Villa Joyosa when someone, whistling jauntily, came down from the small car park, a piece of roughly cleared earth at the end of the road leading from the town.

Mr. Eldridge's whistling stopped abruptly. '*Buenas tardes,*' he greeted Caran, then turned towards the Spaniard. 'I hope it goes well with you, Don Ramiro.'

The difference in appearance between the two men was striking, thought Caran. Don Ramiro in his well-cut dark suit, impeccable shirt and elegant tie, while Brooke Eldridge wore mud-stained jeans, an old grey sweater with strands of wool dangling from a hole in the elbow. His dark red-brown hair stuck up at unruly angles and there was a small streak of mud on his left cheek.

'How is the irrigation going along?' asked Don Ramiro, ignoring Brooke's remark.

'Reasonably well,' answered Brooke. 'That heavy rain a few nights ago did no good at all. Washed away some of the concrete on part of the dam, but no real damage. I suppose you've been helping Miss Ingram to sort out her troubles with these villas? She couldn't hope for anyone better at solving such problems.'

'Don Ramiro was merely interested in seeing the villas, that's all,' Caran put in hastily. She considered that Brooke Eldridge was being unnecessarily rude to Don Ramiro. The words might be innocuous, but the tone they were spoken in was uncivil, to say the least. His manner goaded her to say snappishly, 'We did not even glance at yours. There was no need.'

Brooke nodded pleasantly. 'Thanks. Then I won't detain you. Good night.'

Caran led the way into her own villa, but she was conscious of the fact that Brooke had probably turned his head to see whether Don Ramiro were following her.

'He is not a very pleasant young man,' was Don Ramiro's comment, when he entered the living room. 'But no doubt he will not give you much trouble. If he pays the rent regularly and does no damage, you can leave him alone.'

44

'Has he worked here long on this irrigation construction?' Caran asked as idly as she could.

'More than a year, I believe. But we need waste no more time or thought on the Englishman. Perhaps you would care to have dinner with me in the town?'

Caran was unprepared for this offer—one might almost call it an honour. She had been intending to offer him a snack of some kind, for she knew that the usual dining hour in Spain was about nine o'clock and now the time was barely six. Yet it would be nonsensical to refuse his offer. Don Ramiro was possibly her best chance of acquiring a small measure of influence in Albarosa. With his backing she might manage to stir up the various people concerned with maintenance of the villas.

'If you would give me, say, twenty minutes to dress, I shall be glad to come,' she said demurely.

He smiled 'Only twenty minutes? Most of my women acquaintances need far longer than that to make themselves ready even for a simple meal in a modest Albarosa restaurant.'

As she took a quick shower, then renewed her make-up, she mused on the vast number of womenfolk he must know. Was he married? He had so far made no reference to a wife, but then that was hardly her business. She had not brought an extensive wardrobe with her, intending to buy clothes as she needed them here in Spain. Now she chose a fairly warm dress of midnight blue courtelle with a band of iridescent pearl embroidery at the neck.

When she returned to the living room Don Ramiro displayed his approval of her appearance. 'Only twenty-five minutes,' he said with a glance at his thin gold wrist-watch.

His car was parked near her villa, so Brooke Eldridge must have seen it when he arrived in his own battered estate car. Caran was amused by the thought that Brooke had undoubtedly wanted to see who the visitor was.

Don Ramiro drove swiftly up the winding, narrow road into the town and took her to a café in one of the small squares that she had not so far discovered.

The café was almost full; men on their way home stopped

to meet their friends over coffee or a glass of wine or beer; a couple of families watched their childen eating ice-cream and solitary men read newspapers while they ate, almost absent-mindedly, saucerfuls of *tapas*. Not an apparently obvious English tourist in sight, thought Caran.

This was surely the real Spain where old Moorish customs lingered, for in the streets some of the elderly women still pulled their shawls over their faces at the approach of a stranger. In high summer a sprinkling of tourists would be chattering in their incomprehensible tongues, aiming their cameras at the colourful casbahs or snapping women treading their laundry knee-deep in one of the Moorish fountains.

Don Ramiro asked Caran questions about the villas. 'This woman who owns the group, what is she like?' he wanted to know.

'I don't know very much about her circumstances, except that she's a widow—about fifty, I suppose, or perhaps in her late forties. She has invested most of the capital that her husband left her in these villas and, naturally, wants the investment to pay.'

'Has she ever been here and seen what Albarosa is like?'

'Oh, yes. She told me that she'd spent nearly three months here during the first summer, that was two or three years ago.'

'Then why doesn't she live here permanently and look after her estate?' he asked.

'She has some connection with an antique shop in England and she can't be away for long periods,' Caran told him.

'Then she is not wholly dependent on her income from the villas here?'

Caran shrugged. 'I don't know much about her finances. I expect she told me only what was necessary for me to understand.'

Don Ramiro was silent for a few minutes. Then Caran said, 'I believe you own a villa near Albarosa. Is it far away?'

He smiled. 'You acquire information rapidly. Did Señora Molina tell you?'

'No. Mr. Eldridge mentioned it.'

'Ah, of course, the Englishman. Yes, my villa is on the

other side of Albarosa, on the way to Almeria, but not far. It is shut up at present, but when I open it again, you must come and visit us.'

'Thank you. I'd like to see it.'

When they had dawdled long enough over their aperitifs, Don Ramiro took her on foot through a couple of streets, then a Moorish arch lit with small twinkling lights. A black iron grille opened into a courtyard with high walls and in the centre a small fountain was illuminated by a pale green glow. In warmer weather, Caran supposed, there would be tables out here, but tonight was too chilly.

A door in the corner of the courtyard led down carpeted stairs to a large restaurant decorated in Moorish style with small arches in the ceiling ornamented with the stalactite formation found elsewhere in Andalucia. Tables were ranged around three sides of the floor, leaving a small clear space in the middle, no doubt for dancing, Caran assumed.

She wisely allowed Don Ramiro to select the courses of the entire meal. 'Whatever you order I shall enjoy,' she said.

'Most graciously spoken!' At that moment some trick of the lighting revealed his dark eyes and Caran was aware of a glittering intensity in their depths. She glanced away quickly, slightly disconcerted, but admonishing herself for imagining that Don Ramiro meant any more than a casual compliment.

At the far end of the room a small dais accommodated three musicians, guitar, tambourine and drums. The trio played a variety of Spanish dances and airs but, it seemed to Caran, in a rather listless, bored fashion, until later a pair of flamenco dancers appeared on the space in front of the tables.

The girl wore the red and white spotted Andalucian costume, swinging and twirling so that the many flounces rippled with her movements. There was something familiar to Caran about the girl's face, but she could not place her until almost the end of the dance when she recognized her as Benita, Gabriela's sister. The music rose to a frenzied climax to match the dancers and Benita sank in submission to her masculine conqueror.

The diners applauded, Benita and her partner bowed and the musicians mopped their brows. Clearly they had been

47

saving their energies and enthusiasm for the flamenco exhibition.

'You like our dances?' Don Ramiro asked.

'I haven't seen enough of them to understand the meaning, but I find them thrilling.'

She was undecided whether to disclose to her host that the girl worked in a grocers' shop by day and apparently spent some of her evenings dancing. Caran concluded that what Benita did in her scanty spare time was the latter's business.

Yet as her glance strayed about the restaurant, she saw Benita sitting at a table in a corner near the musicians, and the man opposite was not her partner, but Brooke Eldridge.

Benita was telling him something in a gay, vivacious manner and he listened attentively, now and again adding a word or two when Benita paused for breath. Naturally, thought Caran, he would know Benita quite well during the year he had been in Albarosa. There was no reason why he shouldn't come to this restaurant to dine and watch her dancing.

She wondered, too, if Brooke had seen her in the company of Don Ramiro, but that was less likely, for her host had chosen a table from which dances and any other spectacle could be viewed, while leaving him and Caran in comparative shadow.

Caran tried to keep her glances away from Brooke and his Spanish companion in case the mere act of concentrated staring might induce him to turn his head in her direction, but she was aware of how often her eyes strayed to that corner, although she pretended to watch the musicians.

When she and Don Ramiro rose to leave the restaurant, Brooke was still there, although Benita had disappeared, perhaps to change from her costume into street attire, so that Brooke could accompany her home? After all, Benita lived with her mother, Manuela, quite close to the villas.

Caran resolutely thrust all thoughts of Brooke out of her mind and concentrated on Don Ramiro's suggestion that before he took her back to her villa, they might walk a few yards in the fresh air.

He conducted her along several steep streets, then up one

that was a narrow passage with stone steps. At the top was a white wall with a smooth, rounded top and, looking over it, Caran could see that this point commanded a view over a tremendously wide area.

'We are almost on the top of Albarosa,' he said quietly. 'From here you can see the coast in both directions and some of the mountains. Near here is a tower with a flat roof and from there you can see every point of the compass.'

Glancing below, she could see part of the town, lit in patches while other parts were in darkness. In the moonlight she could distinguish the wide bay with glimpses of white beach. She could not see the villas, for they nestled down by the shore on a lower level and were secluded by bushes and trees, but she could make out the small spit of land close by. Away in the distance towards the west were occasional twinkling lights pricking the dark mass of mountains.

'I didn't realise there were such good viewpoints,' she said. 'I must come up here one time in daylight.'

'Are you then afraid of the dark, even when it is moonlit?' His voice held a caressing, teasing note.

'No, of course not, but what I meant was that if I knew the landscape better in daylight, I'd be able to identify the places better in semi-darkness.'

'Beyond that headland to the left,' he pointed out, 'is a fishing village called Matana. I own some of the land in between; vineyards, olive groves, orange and lemon orchards and so on.'

'So that's why you also have a villa here?'

'You can't see it from here. It's behind a clump of trees over there.' He pointed with a wide sweep of his arm to the right. 'There also I have inherited some of the land.'

'I didn't know you had such important interests in this neighbourhood.' She would not ask him what else he owned in Almeria and the surrounding area. Bringing her to this pinnacle and showing her even part of his kingdom was enough to impress her, but she wondered what exactly were his motives and whether they were connected with her as housekeeper–manager of a few villas, or more personally.

'Gradually Albarosa is changing,' he said. 'When the

49

Moors left most of Spain they were allowed to remain here and keep their customs and traditions. For five centuries they have been content to be isolated even though they are now Christians, not Moslems, and owe allegiance to Spanish rule. Even in my father's time there was no road, only a track across the river beds. Now a better road has come and soon the tourists will discover this town perched on a hill.'

'Is that good or bad?' she asked.

'Both in different ways, perhaps.'

For some minutes he was silent. Then he said, 'You have thought of your position at the villas?'

'My position? How do you mean?'

'Perhaps in your country it is not unusual for a young girl to live alone in a villa while the only other neighbour is a young man?'

Caran laughed softly. 'Oh, you're thinking of the conventions. Mr. Eldridge is at the opposite end to my villa.'

'All the same, until more visitors come, you could consider staying with Señora Molina.'

Caran was firm on this point. 'No. I was engaged to be on the spot. I couldn't keep trudging up and down every day.'

'As you wish.' His tone had become cold.

'Besides,' she continued, 'with Mr. Eldridge there, it's better than being quite alone. If there were any danger——'

He had put unwelcome ideas into her head. What danger could threaten her? If some emergency arose, Brooke would probably not be at home to help her. She dismissed Don Ramiro's scruples. He owned so much of the land around that he could hardly avoid being feudal, with conventions to match.

Long after Caran was home and in bed she heard the sound of a car. Brooke, no doubt. She listened for voices, but if he had brought Benita home, he had already dropped her at her house.

Slightly ashamed that she should be interested in Brooke's late homecoming, she composed herself for sleep. She was not going to let thoughts of either Brooke or Don Ramiro keep her awake.

CHAPTER THREE

CARAN finished her report next morning and walked into the town to post it. She hoped Mrs. Parmenter would understand that the villas could not be set in apple-pie order ready for letting without the money being available.

Today the sky was overcast and she was more than half-way home down the road to the villas when a few spots of rain fell. She began to run, but not fast enough to escape the sharp shower that soaked her hair and the lightweight coat she was wearing.

A car hooted behind her and she moved to the side of the road to avoid being splashed any more than was necessary.

'Going far?' bawled the driver, as he leaned out of the window. He was already opening the door on the off side.

She might have known that few people other than Brooke would be using this road, but there was no point in getting wetter, so she shook the raindrops off her coat and clambered into the estate car.

'Sorry I didn't pick you up before the shower,' he said blandly. 'I didn't realise you'd be out and about after your evening out.'

'I wasn't very late coming home,' she said mildly, and was about to say 'Not as late as you', but stopped herself in time. That would have been a give-away, indeed.

He swung the car expertly into the car-park and she prepared to alight, but he put out a restraining hand.

'Wait a few moments. The rain will stop very soon.'

Certainly it was coming down in buckets and she closed the car door.

'You're going it a bit with the noble Don, aren't you?' he said, after a pause.

'What do you mean by that?' Her resentment was quickly aroused.

'Only that Don Ramiro isn't usually lavish or casual with his invitations to dinner.'

'At least he has good manners,' she pointed out.

'In which I'm lacking—oh, I know. I'm only trying to warn you that he usually has strong motives. He's the calculating type. Nothing impulsive about him.'

'That doesn't mean that his motives are necessarily bad ones,' she countered. She turned towards Brooke. 'And could I remind you that you warned me not to pry or spy on you? You seem to have kept a close watch on all my movements.'

He laughed. 'Are you pretending that you didn't see me in the restaurant, the Marroqui? Several times you looked straight at me.'

'I might have been wondering whether you had deliberately followed Don Ramiro and me or whether it was mere coincidence that you happened to dine in the same restaurant.'

'I was there first, as it happened. I saw you and Don Ramiro come in, but I was much too discreet to wave to you both in my vulgar fashion.'

'The rain has nearly stopped now.' She unfastened the door and stepped out of the car. 'Thank you for the lift.'

'Did he offer any help about finding accommodation for Gabriela and her brood?' Brooke leaned towards the door.

'M'm. He'll manage something,' Caran murmured vaguely, unwilling to admit that she had not taken up the question again or that she was not sure if any kind of help were in Don Ramiro's power.

She hurried off to her own villa before Brooke could ask any further awkward questions. Besides, she wanted to read the letters she had collected at the post office. There was no delivery service down here at the villas and all correspondence and parcels had to be posted or collected in the town. She assumed that Brooke had always attended to his own mail.

One was from her mother, hoping that Caran had found everything in order and was enjoying her new job in lovely winter sunshine. 'Here, it rains non-stop every day,' she wrote, 'but if it were fine, I should probably be out in the garden all the time, so I have to catch up with odd jobs indoors.'

Caran's mother was an ardent gardener and won prizes and cups in local horticultural shows. Winter sunshine! Well, at this time of year one couldn't expect the sun to shine every day, thought Caran, as she dried her soaked hair with a thick towel.

Her mother had enclosed two other letters from friends who did not know Caran was in Spain. The bulky envelope Caran had left until last, for she recognised Julie's untidy scrawl. There were several sheets written on both sides and Caran waded through an account of the shortcomings of Julie's new boy-friend, troubles at the photographic studio where she worked and the difficulty of finding a suitable flat-mate to replace Caran.

'So I thought I'd have a holiday from everything (Julie wrote), and come and spend a couple of weeks or so with you. I remember you said that some of the villas were empty, so you could probably fix me up. I'm giving up this flat at the end of the month, so I've got to find somewhere else and it might as well be a warm and sunny place where I can be idle and away from it all. Let me know quickly, won't you? Have you met any interesting men yet?

'Love, Julie.'

Caran walked around the living room with the letter in her hand. How was she to reply to Julie? It was not that she wanted to deprive the other girl of a holiday, but she had no authority to let villas to casual friends. The best solution might be to let Julie share Caran's own villa.

She read the letter again. Julie spoke of giving up the flat at the end of the month. It was now the second week of November, so that left little time for delay, unless Julie meant she would come later in December or even after Christmas. Knowing Julie's impulsiveness and her partiality for snap decisions, Caran concluded that her friend wanted a speedy reply to facilitate a speedy departure.

After lunch Caran spent the afternoon answering her

letters, telling Julie that she would welcome her and asking for the exact date when she would be coming. She also wrote to Mrs. Parmenter explaining the situation and offering to find Julie accommodation in the town if there was any objection to her staying in an unoccupied villa.

When she returned from the town after posting the letters, Caran called on Gabriela.

'I must have the other bed returned,' she instructed.

Gabriela looked blank. 'But what shall I do if I have not enough beds for the children?'

Caran tried to be reasonable and patient with this woman who certainly had her troubles, but yet wore them like a crown of thorns. 'Listen, Gabriela, you must have had some beds and furniture in the place where you lived before you came here.'

'No, no—all gone to buy food.'

Caran winced at this example of such abject poverty.

'But your husband——' she began.

'Felipe is working now and he works hard at El Catalan, but for a few months before then he was ill and could not work at all. That was why we could not pay the rent.'

Caran was silent. 'Well, I shall do my best to get you another place, but you must also help yourselves and look for something. Ask your husband, Felipe, to come and see me when he has free time.'

Gabriela promised to do so, adding that she would walk all the streets of Albarosa to find even a barn or stable where the family could live, but how was she to do so with so many children clutching her skirts? 'I could not leave them here alone and my mother cannot attend to all of them.'

Caran conceded the point and left Gabriela to her endless household chores of washing, cleaning and cooking.

The next morning Felipe appeared at the door of Caran's villa with the divan base of a single bed.

'*Señorita*,' he said politely, 'here is part and I go to bring the rest.' He propped the base in the porch and went away, returning in a few minutes with the mattress on his head and the headboard under his arm.

'Thank you, Felipe. Would you mind bringing the whole

lot into the bedroom?'

Gabriela's husband was fairly tall and slender. His thin dark face showed permanent anxiety, two deep lines were etched either side of his straight Latin nose, and the much-mended trousers and thin sweater he wore this morning were hardly enough to keep out the chilly wind. It probably took him effort enough to dress respectably in his waiter's clothes and off duty he had nothing but this shabby outfit.

When the extra bed was in position in Caran's bedroom, she asked him to sit down and gave him a glass of wine.

At the end of the long conversation he admitted that he was no nearer finding another place to live than he had been six or seven weeks ago. There was nothing he could afford. Yet Caran had the impression that he was not only honest, but eager to get away and make a more settled life for his wife and family.

'When the villas are let, I could possibly employ Gabriela to do some of the cleaning,' she offered. 'Benita, too, could come back as a maid.'

His face lit up with grateful smiles and he grasped her hand. 'Yes, yes, all will come right for us and we will all work hard,' he promised.

That evening she thought it would be a friendly gesture if she dined at El Catalan where Felipe served her with an excellent meal and she gave him a generous tip.

Nearly a week went by and she had heard nothing from Mrs. Parmenter. Without more money to oil the wheels, Caran felt she was at a standstill as far as encouraging the painters and workmen to resume their operations.

So far there was not enough for her to do, although she realised that when the season really started she would probably be run off her feet without a minute to spare. One afternoon she roamed along the shore on the far side of Albarosa. Don Ramiro had indicated that his villa was somewhere in that direction, but when she came to the limit of the sandy beach backed by clusters of pines there was nothing but rocky stone outcrops and after a few difficult climbs up and down, she turned back.

Almost as soon as she entered the villa, a man's voice

called out, 'Miss Ingram! Are you at home?'

She hastened to open the door. The man standing in the porch was vaguely familiar.

'I'm Paul,' he announced. 'Aunt Alison's nephew—Mrs. Parmenter, you know.'

'Oh, of course. Come in.' She had glimpsed him only hurriedly at the airport and had not been prepared for his sudden appearance here.

'You got my aunt's letter telling you I was on my way?' he asked.

'No. I went to the post office this morning, but there was nothing there from Mrs. Parmenter.'

'Oh, bad luck. Never mind. I'm here, so that's all right. I'll leave all my gear out here in the porch.'

'What sort of meal would you like?' she asked. 'English or Spanish? We could have tea and toast or coffee and cakes or I could cook you something more substantial. Are you hungry?'

'Not particularly. English tea and toast sounds good on this November afternoon. Not that it's really cold weather. In this part of Spain it never becomes icy, except in the mountains, but somehow you always expect Spain to be sunny and warm and fit for lying about basking in the sun.'

While he drank tea and ate the fingers of toast and little scones that Caran had made this morning, she studied Paul Fernwood. Medium height and rather stocky in build, fair hair and a pale face inclined to fleshiness; even in his tweed suit he looked very much the business type, as though he ought always to be wearing a bowler hat and carrying a rolled umbrella.

'Aunt Alison thought that I'd better come for a while and see if I could help you to straighten out matters. Also, it fitted in quite well with my own plans, so here I am.'

She told him briefly what she had already reported to Mrs. Parmenter. 'All the workmen say no credit.'

'We'll soon put that right,' he promised.

After tea, she asked if he had made arrangements for accommodation in the town or was he intending to stay temporarily in one of the villas.

'Oh, I thought I could take one of the spare villas for the time being,' he answered.

'In that case I'll go and attend to it, see that it's aired and so on.'

'I'll take the one next door,' he suggested. 'Then it's easy for us to be in touch.'

Caran knew now that she could no longer delay admitting that one villa was unlawfully occupied. Paul would soon find out for himself.

'I didn't put it in the report,' she confessed, 'because I thought I might solve that problem in a short time, but you'd better know about it now.'

Paul listened to her account of Gabriela's circumstances. Then he said cheerfully, 'Oh, don't worry, Caran—I hope I may call you that? Don't worry, we'll soon turf them out. If we don't, they'll invite their friends to come and take over any other villas that happen to be empty.'

Caran was vaguely disquieted. Perhaps she should already have been firmer with the family, but Paul sounded as if he were quite prepared to use strong-arm tactics.

For the next hour she was busy attending to the Villa Turquesa, next to her own, and making it comfortable for Paul.

'It's a little dusty,' she apologised, 'but I'll get it cleaned out properly in the morning.'

'There should be at least one maid here to look after all the villas. What's happened to that girl?—Benita, I think her name was.'

'She's working at a shop in the town. Evidently she didn't get paid her wages.'

'Oh, that blessed agent we used. He seems to have let the whole place go to pot.'

Caran smiled. 'That's why I gather your aunt wanted someone on the spot.' At the same time, she was now beginning to wonder why Paul hadn't come in the first place to act as a resident manager. Perhaps he had an important job in London and could be absent for only a limited time.

Back in Caran's villa, she and Paul studied the copy of her report, item by item. She made notes of his comments and

57

instruction.

'You know all this part quite well, I suppose? Were you here in the summer?' she queried.

'Yes, I stayed a few weeks. I was glad I did, for I saw various possibilities here. When I came the previous year I wasn't in the right mood to enjoy myself. My fiancée had just thrown me over—and there were other problems.'

'I'm sorry—about your broken engagement, I mean. Not mended yet?'

'Indeed, no. She's married someone else.'

Caran nodded and gave a little sigh to indicate that she understood just how disrupting women could be to a man's life. She guessed that he might be about twenty-five or six, so there was probably plenty of time for him to meet the right girl.

'Let's go up to the town and have dinner, shall we?' he suggested when they came to the end of the report.

'I'd like that,' she agreed in what she hoped was a businesslike non-committal tone without too much eagerness.

He ordered a taxi to take them into Albarosa. 'I'll have to see about hiring a car while I'm here,' he said. 'Do you drive?'

'I've no experience of driving on Continental roads,' she admitted hastily. 'At home I drove my father's car but I'd need a little practice in keeping to the right instead of the left.' She smiled. 'Why do the British have to be so individual?'

He chose El Catalan for dinner, but Caran could not see Felipe. Perhaps it was his night off duty.

Halfway through the meal, Paul raised his glass of wine to Caran. 'Here's to our partnership!' he said, his grey eyes sparkling with cordiality. 'Oh, I can see we're going to get along famously.'

Caran was slightly bewildered by the speed with which Paul Fernwood established so amicable a footing. She herself was accustomed to progress more gradually in her acquaintanceships. Julie, for instance, was entirely opposite, falling over herself with enthusiasm for new friends, then as speedily discovering their faults. It occurred to Caran to mention Julie now.

'A friend—we shared a flat in London—wants to come for a short holiday,' she explained. 'Would it be all right if she shared my villa?'

'Certainly. Why not?' Paul agreed. 'I expect you could do with a little bit of English company. By the way, have you met our resident recluse, Eldridge?'

A faint flush spread over Caran's face and she hoped Paul would not notice it. 'Oh, yes, I met him as soon as I came here.' That was entirely true.

'Queer fish, isn't he? Likes to put up a notice, as it were, "Keep out!" Still, we don't mind. He occupies a villa all the year round and that's one useful rent. Of course, if the time comes, as I hope it will, when all our villas are let right through the year, we shall put his villa to better use or put up the rent.'

Caran allowed this prospective threat to slide by. Brooke Eldridge might have finished his work on the irrigation scheme by that time.

'I gather he works here on irrigation,' she remarked.

'Somewhere up in the hills. Free and easy sort of job, apparently, for I believe he goes off pottering about the district for days at a time.'

'Maybe he studies other irrigation schemes elsewhere,' she suggested. 'Compares notes.'

Paul laughed derisively. 'Compares notes about the girls, more likely. Oh, I know he pretends here that he's not interested in feminine society, but that's probably a blind.'

'Oh, I didn't know,' she murmured lamely. Then she tried to draw the conversation around to Gabriela and Felipe. 'The husband, Felipe, works here as a waiter, although he's apparently not here tonight. If we could find them somewhere else to go, they'd be off like a shot. They're very proud and independent, and it's only sheer bad luck and illness and so on that's brought them to their present plight.'

'One must never waste too much sympathy with people of that kind,' he said curtly. 'They just take advantage of any consideration.'

'I'm sure this family would not. I told Don Ramiro——'

'Don Ramiro?' he echoed. 'The Mendosa fellow?'

'Yes, I——'

'Then you've already made his acquaintance? How?'

Caran recounted how Don Ramiro had driven her from Granada and lodged her with one of his friends partly because of the late hour of arrival, partly on account of the flooded path.

'The wily old devil!' murmured Paul softly. 'I wonder how he knew you were coming.'

'But surely he couldn't know. Anyway, why would it matter?'

Paul chuckled. 'There isn't much that goes on in Albarosa that the good Don Ramiro doesn't know. He has his spies everywhere.'

'For what purpose?' asked Caran.

'Oh, he regards himself as Albarosa's feudal lord. He owns large estates around here.'

'Yes, he showed me some of the land he owns.'

Paul's needle glance immediately warned her that her remark had been incautious. 'Then you've seen him again? Since you arrived?'

She nodded. 'He came one afternoon to look at the villas.'

'He would. What was his impression?'

'He criticised the structure, said it was shoddy and so on, but all the same he promised to help in various ways—to get the workmen to come and—perhaps—find a place for Gabriela and Felipe.'

'That was handsome of him!' Paul spoke with derision.

'Have I done something wrong in becoming acquainted with Don Ramiro?' she asked. Apprehension of disastrous consequences made her voice tremble slightly. 'In the first place, I'd no option about letting him drive me here, other than staying the night in Granada. I'd no idea at all who he was. I thought he was just a car-driver going my way.'

Paul was silent for a few moments. He rocked the wine in his glass so that the restaurant lights caught in its crimson glow.

His silence now disconcerted her, for she was already abashed by the fact that so early in her employment he had been forced to come. 'I know you've had to come here to straighten out the tangles, but that was mostly due to money problems,' she said defensively. 'I could have coped quite well apart from the bills.'

Paul glanced up and gave her a warm smile. Then he stretched out his hand and lightly placed it over hers. 'Caran, my girl, your meeting with Don Ramiro is the most fortunate thing in the world. Between us, we shall be well on the way to becoming millionaires.'

Between us? Who did that include? Himself and Don Ramiro? Or did he mean to include her in a trio of capitalists? This latter possibility caused her to laugh spontaneously at the fantastic idea.

He joined her in laughter, unaware that they were laughing for probably quite different reasons.

The next few days were extremely busy while Paul chased up the various workmen and Caran attended to all the correspondence. Paul's Spanish was only roughly conversational and it was left to Caran to struggle with the dictionary or the niceties of Spanish grammar.

On some evenings Paul took her to dinner in the town at one of the restaurants; at other times they stayed at home and Caran cooked a simple meal for the two of them.

Paul, she noticed, was the kind of man who sat in the living room and read the newspaper while the cooking was going on. Brooke would have come uninvited into the kitchen, lifting pot lids and sniffing appreciatively or critically. He'd probably tell her what was wrong or insist on adding a dash of this or that seasoning.

Although he had been at Albarosa so short a time, Paul had drifted into the casual habit of kissing Caran good night in a rather absent-minded manner or walking about the villa gardens with his arm about her waist. She was not particularly disturbed by these slight atttentions, for she regarded him as at least her deputy boss, since he was Mrs. Parmenter's nephew.

Yet one occasion caused her a certain uneasiness. She and Paul had alighted from his hired car which he parked at the back of the villas. As they walked down the steps into the gardens, Paul suddenly swung her towards him in a close embrace, kissed her cheek, then the corner of her mouth. Then, still with his arm around her waist, he called cheerily, 'Hallo there, Eldridge!'

Brooke was coming towards them, probably on his way to the car parking space. He nodded briefly as he passed and his face was unsmiling.

Caran flushed, realising that Paul had deliberately intended Brooke to see him on familiar terms with her. She was more than willing to be on amicable terms with Paul; in fact, it was in her own best interests. At the same time she objected to becoming a piece of property that Paul could flaunt whenever he chose.

She was not displeased when a day or two after the incident Paul returned from collecting the mail at the post office and handed her a telegram addressed to herself.

'My friend Julie is coming tomorrow,' she told him.

Julie would at least provide a diversion for Paul if only on a temporary basis.

'Tomorrow,' he repeated thoughtfully. 'Did you tell her to stay the night at Granada and come on here the next day?'

'No. I wasn't sure of the date she was coming.'

Typical of Julie, thought Caran, to give the shortest possible notice of her intended visit. At the same time, Caran blamed herself for not pointing out the difficulties of transport at this time of year.

Paul smiled. 'We can't depend on Don Ramiro to be at the airport a second time and convey our passengers to Albarosa. I'd better meet her at Granada and drive her here.'

'No need for that, surely.' Caran was conscious of the time Paul would waste, most of a day and evening. 'I can telegraph her to stay in Granada for the night. Which hotel would you recommend?'

'I stayed at the Nevada Palace. She'd be all right there.'

Caran wrote out a telegram, but then it occurred to her that she did not know if Julie was still at the flat. 'I can send it to the airport at Granada.'

Paul looked dubious. 'Look, all this is more trouble than my going to meet her. What's she like? Young and pretty?'

'Both,' Caran agreed. 'She's about average height, has an animated face and the most glorious reddish-gold hair.'

'M'm. Sounds a dish.'

'She needs to be. She's a photographer's model—advertising and all that.'

Caran had been almost on the point of offering to accompany Paul on the day trip, so that there would be no difficulty in identifying Julie, but now she hesitated. It was quite obvious that he wanted the zest of meeting a new girl visitor. Perhaps since his broken engagement he was ever on the look-out for a girl who might adequately replace his lost fiancée. For all Caran knew, he might even be sizing her up.

After Paul had left the villa and she was alone ostensibly busy with the correspondence, she stopped typing and allowed her thoughts to roam. Paul was attractive in many ways with his cheerful personality, his sharp business acumen that would undoubtedly steer him towards reasonable wealth, yet she could not acknowledge to herself that she was attracted to the man. Somewhere underneath his brisk, genial exterior was an elusive quality that she could not identify, a ruthless indifference to the hurts he might inflict on others.

Besides, Caran told herself, she could hardly accompany him to Granada, even if he had asked her. Someone had to stay here at the villas to see that the workmen carried out their instructions.

When Paul set off next morning on the long journey to Granada, Caran saw him off and waved as his car climbed the road. 'You can't miss her!' she had told him a few moments ago. 'Julie shines like a candle flame in a dark room.'

As she walked back to her villa, she smiled to herself, wondering what impact Paul and Julie would have on each other. This was something that would have to emerge in the next few days and in the meantime, there was work to do this morning.

She had to tackle Brooke Eldridge on a delicate mission. Would he please move out of his villa for two or three days and occupy one of the others while his own, the Zafiro, was repainted?

Caran wrote the politest little note, for she assumed he would not be at home until the evening. She looked in first at the Villa Esmeralda where two Spaniards were applying white paint to the outside walls. As she called a greeting, one stepped back hastily and upset his bucket of paint all over the floor of the porch.

'Oh, quickly!' she cried. 'Clean it up quickly or it will spoil the floor.'

'*Si, señorita*,' said the man unhurriedly. '*Momento.*' He dabbed at the floor with a cloth little larger than a handkerchief and Caran became impatient. 'You should have a *fregadero grande*,' she said, hoping she was using the right word for 'mop', but the man smiled charmingly, went round a corner of the villa and reappeared with a bucket of dirty water and what looked like a bundle of rags tied to a stick.

'All will be clean in three minutes,' he told her. 'Come back and see, *señorita*.'

In the most delicately polite manner he was dismissing her so that she should see the result of his labours and not the questionable methods.

She smiled at the man and took the hint. 'I'll come back later,' she promised. She walked down to the main path that connected the villas and up towards Brooke's. As she rounded a magnolia tree she heard voices and a moment later saw Benita in her flamenco costume apparently posing while Brooke took photographs.

Caran stood still, not wishing to interrupt the proceedings, but Brooke swung round, camera in hand. 'Oh, come on, Caran, if you're coming! You've distracted Benita anyway and she's changed her expression.'

'I'm terribly sorry about that,' Caran said coolly. 'I didn't mean to barge in.'

Benita, in her red and white spotted flounced dress, seemed rather apprehensive and on the point of flight.

'All right, Benita,' said Brooke in Spanish. 'You can go now. I've probably taken all the photographs I want.'

The girl picked up her flowing skirts and ran down the

path.

'You needn't have dismissed her like that merely because I came on the scene,' objected Caran.

'Why not?' His piercing blue eyes demanded a sensible answer. 'I suppose I'm the best judge of how many photographs I want to take.'

'Of course,' agreed Caran. It was an unfortunate beginning to her morning's errand when she had to ask him a favour. 'I suppose Benita has the morning off from her work in the shop?' She made the remark merely to gain time and put off explaining the real reason for her call.

Brooke, who had been replacing his camera in its case, now looked up suddenly. 'Does her absence there inconvenience you?'

'No. Why should it?'

He gave her that slightly lopsided smile that meant he was trying to score off her or that he was amused by her discomfiture.

'Do you also want to know why I'm not working this morning?'

'I'm not curious about it,' she retorted.

'Splendid. I wondered what excuse I'd be able to give you apart from fooling around with Benita for an hour or two.'

'Mr. Eldridge——' she began with what dignity she could summon.

'Oh, you were calling me Brooke a few days ago. Why this formal address, or is it meant to be a most formal call?'

'Yes, I came with a purpose,' she told him.

'I didn't believe you were making a spontaneous call because you longed for the sight of me.'

'Would you mind listening?' Her voice had become icy and she regretted it, but the way he goaded her was beyond endurance.

'Go ahead. Perhaps you'd like to step inside. It's rather chilly out here this morning.'

That, of course, was a two-edged remark indicating her manner as well as the weather, but she made no answer.

His sitting room was littered with papers and books everywhere and he swept a pile off one of the easy chairs so that she could sit down.

'A glass of wine to warm you?' he offered.

She shook her head. 'No, thank you.' She was almost tempted to rush out of the villa and say she'd come another day, but the matter of the repainting was becoming urgent. What should have been no more than an incidental request had now become inflated into a tiresome, formal interview.

'I want to ask you a favour,' she began, thus putting herself in the position of one who makes a request, without appearing to compel.

'Yes?' His oblique glance revealed a suspicious wariness.

'As you know, we are repainting all the villas——'

'I saw that you'd persuaded the workmen to start again. Was that due to the efforts of the redoubtable Paul Fernwood?'

'Perhaps it was. He brought the money to pay the bills,' she snapped. 'Would you be prepared to move out of your villa into one of the others, so that yours can be redecorated?'

'Move out!' he echoed, turning away and thrusting his hands in his trouser pockets. 'I couldn't possibly collect all this stuff and take it somewhere else and then hope to lay hands on it again! Quite impossible! In any case,' he swung back towards her, 'does it matter whether the Zafiro is painted sapphire blue or any other colour? I'm the only one who lives in it. I rent it permanently, so why should you worry if the walls are none to clean?'

'We should prefer not to have one of the villas looking really shabby,' she pointed out quietly.

'You mean I might be letting down the side? Well, that's too bad. If I prefer my own brand of chaos, that's my business. You get my cheque for the rent regularly on the first of every month and you must let me stew in my appalling untidiness.'

'You're very unco-operative,' she grumbled. 'We would undertake to have the job done very quickly indeed for you.'

He laughed harshly. 'Oh, I know what would happen. The men would start, then for some reason, they'd be shifted elsewhere and there I'd be with the work half done and with no prospect of ever getting straight again.'

Caran rose. 'There's no point in arguing, then, Mr. Eldridge,' she said stiffly. 'I'll tell Paul that you refuse point blank to be disturbed.'

Brooke grinned. 'Is that a threat that you'll send him along to put a pistol at my head?'

Caran smiled coldly. 'He might have more persuasive powers than I have.'

'And why didn't our brave Paul come this morning or at least accompany you?'

'He's gone to Granada to meet a friend of mine,' Caran replied.

'Friend? Masculine or feminine? No, that's a silly question. Obviously feminine gender. Only women are met at Granada and conveyed here. Men have to fend for themselves in hired cars. In any case, Paul would never bother to drive all that way to meet another man.'

'How well do you know Paul?' she asked.

'Oh, he's been here at various times,' Brooke answered indifferently. 'Poked his nose in here a day or two ago to see if I was still surviving or if I'd met a watery grave up in the hills on the dam.'

'I'll be going now,' Caran reminded him. 'If you change your mind about the repainting, perhaps you'll let me know.'

She was walking towards the outer door when the edge of her skirt caught on a pile of photographs and the whole batch slithered to the floor.

'I'm sorry about that,' she apologised, stooping to pick them up.

'No damage done.' He knelt to gather the scattered glossy prints. 'No damage, that is, to these. But I can see that the whole sordid story is now going to come tumbling out.'

She could see that many of the photographs were those of girls or women in various Spanish costumes; others depicted processions, landscapes or odd corners of villages.

With a gracious gesture she handed him back half a dozen photographs. 'I never probe if I can help it or force an unwilling confidence,' she said sententiously.

67

Brooke sat back on his heels and rocked with laughter. 'But you're dying to know all the same. In any case, I shall insist on telling you.'

'Don't make me a party to any of your iniquities!' she mocked.

'Quiet! I'm trying to write a book on some of the lesser-known Spanish fiestas and customs. The processions and so on. Everyone knows about those in Seville or Barcelona, but there are any amount in small towns and villages all over Spain. Soon many of them will disappear for lack of support, so I had the idea of including them in a book with as many photographs as the publisher will stand.'

'And you were photographing Benita for that purpose?'

'Not at all. I want her picture as one of my pin-ups. Besides, that costume is not really her local dress. She just wears that rig-out for her flamenco dancing. But of course, you've seen her.'

'Once.'

He stared at her in mock surprise. 'Do you mean to tell me that our hero Paul hasn't taken you to the Marroqui? I know that Don Ramiro escorted you there.'

'Paul and I just haven't time to keep going into the town for dinner and entertainment,' she said brusquely.

He bent his head to one side and regarded her with mocking curiosity. 'I'm all agog to know how you spend the evenings then. Little intimate dinners by candlelight with Paul? And afterwards, I suppose, you pore over the accounts together? Or do you sit side by side and read poetry?'

She was now so angry that she was forced to laugh. Otherwise, she might have slapped his face and that would have proved that she was really riled.

'It's fatal to judge other people by your own standards and tastes,' she said sweetly. 'Yes, Paul and I do usually have dinner together in my villa and I cook it. Nothing elaborate, you understand.'

Brooke sighed gustily. 'Some men just fall feet first into the lap of luxury and take their cushioned ease as though they had a right to it. You never offered to cook a dinner for me.'

'Oh, I couldn't hope to please you,' she said testily. 'You'd criticise and find fault with everything.'

'Here am I, condemned to solitary snacks that I can knock up at home or else forced to eat in restaurants up in the town. Invite me one night and let's have a sample of your *cordon bleu.*'

'I'm not going to be ordered whom to invite,' she retorted. 'Wait until you're asked. Besides, I understand you liked being undisturbed and left alone to your own devices.'

'So I did. So I do!' he corrected himself hastily.

'That's all right, then,' she said smugly. 'If you change your mind, I'll send my friend along to you. She's young, pretty and gay.'

'And not weighed down by the cares of these establishments. Pity that a little bit of responsibility makes you so difficult, Caran.'

'Difficult? That makes two of us. You're the man who won't move out of his villa for a couple of days while it's repainted.' She turned towards the porch. *'Adios!'*

There was no answering farewell and Caran had walked a few paces down the path. 'Hi! I've changed my mind about that!' Brooke called in a loud voice. 'If you'll supply me with the paint and brushes and so on, I'll do it myself.'

'Are you capable?' she shouted back, for she was now some distance away.

'Immensely! You'll be envious when you see the result. Besides, think of the money I'll save you.'

'All right,' she agreed, and hurried off down the path.

Brooke Eldridge was quite impossible with his 'blow hot, blow cold' moods. Quite probably in a day or so he would back out of his promise to do his own decorations. The only way to cope with him was to accept him at any moment as he happened to be, expansive or playing the hermit as he chose.

Caran had more important concerns to attend to today in Paul's absence. She had already wasted too much time on Brooke this morning and she had to make preparations for Julie's visit.

CHAPTER FOUR

'It was really very deceitful of you, Caran, to keep quiet about all these exciting men you've met!' complained Julie a couple of days after her arrival.

The two girls were sunning themselves in the porch of the Villa Joyosa.

'What should I have done?' asked Caran, with an amused smile. 'Written you a precise report on them, describing their appearance, their jobs, their prospects? Besides, when you say "all these men", you make it sound as though I've met half an army instead of a couple.'

'Oh, I wouldn't put it past you to have another couple up your sleeve with notices—"Strictly reserved".'

'You mean reserved for Julie?' Caran laughed. 'Actually, I'll spill a secret. I *have* an extremely handsome Spanish Don tucked away in my sleeve.' She thrust out her bare arm. She was wearing a sleeveless dress.

Julie sighed mockingly. 'For a girl who's never really gone overboard for a man, you've hotted up the pace.'

'And how would you know who might have tempted me overboard, as you call it?'

'Darling, you can always tell by a girl's face when she's in love.'

'All right. Next time you start raving about your latest conquest, I shall study your face very carefully and see what I can learn.'

By the time Julie had stayed in Albarosa for little more than a week, it was evident that she had made a tremendous impact on Paul. Instant victory, Caran termed it.

In fact, since the girl's arrival, he had spent most of his time taking Julie out and about for trips to Almeria or Murcia, up the Sierras or down to little fishing villages along the coast. Usually they came home very late and Julie would explain that Paul had taken her to dinner at some delectable place along the route home.

'I know I'm monopolising him, pet,' she apologised one night as she crept into her own bed in the room she shared with Caran, 'but don't grudge me my little hour. It's not for long. Soon I'll be back to the grind.'

'Of course I don't grudge you,' murmured Caran sleepily. 'Anyway, Paul isn't my property.'

'No, he isn't.' Julie's decisive tone precluded argument. After a pause she said, 'You have your compensation in the Eldridge man.'

Caran pretended to be asleep and did not reply, but in the darkness she smiled. Julie had met Brooke Eldridge only briefly the day after she had arrived and since then he had been away for several days, either on his working site or on one of those mysterious trips that he took from time to time.

Mysterious they might appear to Paul and others, but Caran now knew that Brooke's absences were on account of the small fiestas taking place all the year round in one or another village or minor town. This was a confidence that, although discovered by accident, she would not divulge.

Paul in any case was not distressed by Brooke's non-appearance for several days. 'I suppose he has a girl-friend or two somewhere up in the mountains or at one of the villages along the coast, but I wouldn't care if he never came back.'

Caran smiled and said nothing. 'I'm sorry, though,' Paul continued, 'to leave you to cope with all the business details as they crop up, but you're quite capable now of handling almost anything here. I feel I must show Julie as much of this part of Spain while she's here. You understand that, don't you?'

'Of course,' agreed Caran.

'Actually, she could be a splendid advertisement for us and the villas when she gets home. Personal inspection and all that, you see. By the way, is she staying over Christmas?'

'I don't know. Have you asked her?'

Paul looked across the garden for a moment. 'No, but I'll do so.' He turned towards Caran with a sudden smile. 'After she goes back, we'll do some trips out together, you and I. How would that be?'

'Fine,' answered Caran in as even a tone as she could manage. So she was to be picked up and taken for car drives and outings when Julie was no longer there. Paul didn't mean to be patronising. It was merely his way of trying to be kind.

'I must see if Julie's ready,' muttered Paul. As he went towards the Villa Joyosa, Julie strolled out to the porch and stood there for a moment as though she were posing for a photographer. Evidently Paul thought so, too.

'Hold it a moment while I get my camera!' he called, and rushed away towards his own villa.

Certainly Julie looked worth any amount of film this morning in a new dress of cream wool trimmed with emerald green pockets and scarf.

'Very smart,' commented Caran.

Julie gurgled with laughter. 'The dress? Or do you mean my effect on Paul?'

Caran laughed. 'I was talking about the dress, but I see what you mean.'

'Technique,' murmured Julie, putting a hand to her lovely red-gold hair. 'Merely a matter of knowing when to switch on—or off, darling. You should try using it some time.'

'I'm always willing to learn,' Caran said spiritedly.

But then Paul was back again, checking his exposure meter and posing Julie in the most advantageous positions.

Caran knew when she was one too many. 'Goodbye, both of you!' she called. 'Have a pleasant day.'

She hurried down the path away from the villas and walked along the rough, stony strip of land above the golden beach. She stared at the sea, green as a peridot this morning, and the high, light clouds above. How fortunate it was that she had not lost her heart to Paul, or she would have been raving jealous of Julie's possessive attitude.

On her return she decided to inspect the two new villas in process of being built and see what progress had been made.

A dozen workmen busied themselves with cement-mixing, fixing windows or plastering inside walls. Both roofs were on, in one case a flat roof to form an extra patio. At the moment there was no balustrade and Caran hoped no one would carelessly step over the edge into space.

She discussed a few details with the foreman in charge of

the buildings, asking questions as to completion and receiving emphatic answers that everything would be speedy.

'With never a *mañana* to be heard,' she reflected.

There were several matters that Paul must attend to, chiefly financial, and Caran was on her way back to the other villas to write down her notes before she forgot them, when Brooke suddenly appeared on the path.

'Oh, you've come back, I see, she remarked.

'Did you miss me, then?'

'Not really. I've had other things to do.' She gave him a friendly grin.

'Where's your luscious-looking friend this morning?'

'Out with Paul somewhere,' she replied.

'And that pair have gone off and left you? Poor little Miss Lonely Heart!'

'Spare me your pity, please,' she begged. 'Julie is here for a holiday and doesn't want to spend it all outside the porch of our villa.'

'True.' He nodded. He broke off a dead leaf from a yucca. 'Busy today?'

'Not particularly. I've just inspected the two new villas and I've a few notes to make about those.'

'Right. Then how would you like to come with me to a little village along the coast? Today is one of their pre-Christmas festivals and I'd like to see what goes on.'

Caran hesitated. Was she justified in Paul's absence in leaving all the villas without supervision?

Brooke misread her hesitation. 'What frightens you? The idea of spending a day with me? You trusted Don Ramiro, didn't you? And that was in the dark. What about Paul? You go all over the place with him. Or rather, you did until your delightful friend arrived and shoved your nose out of joint.'

Caran made up her mind. 'So my nose is out of joint, is it? Very well, Mr. Eldridge, I'll be glad to come out with you, if it's only to prove that your assumptions are quite incorrect.'

'I see. All right, I'll accept you on the rebound, since the ball's in my court. How long do you take to get ready?'

'Ten minutes or so.'

'Make it ten minutes and forget the rest,' he advised, 'or I shall set off without you. I don't want to miss half the show.'

'Any more remarks like that and I shall definitely decide to stay at home!'

He put his hand on her shoulder and gave her a little push. 'Don't get uppish or bad-tempered. You're not the one with red hair.'

She was about to make some further retort, but he gave her a second gentle push. 'Save it for another time,' he murmured.

In her villa she noted with dismay the untidy state of her bedroom. Julie's clothes were strewn on the beds, on chairs, on the floor. A white sandal hung halfway out of a suitcase and a dressing-wrap lay crumpled inside the open wardrobe.

Caran had been aware of Julie's untidiness during the time they had shared a flat, but then they had not also shared a bedroom.

Now she hurriedly hung a few garments in the wardrobe, put the shoes away and attended to her own appearance. Even then, Brooke's patience appeared to be minimal, for in a few minutes he was shouting from the porch.

'Don't be so impatient!' she shouted back, thrusting her feet into more sturdy sandals, for she guessed that today's outing might involve a good deal of walking.

'I'd better leave a note for Paul,' she said when she joined Brooke, who was now prowling restlessly around the porch.

'Why? Will he expect you to be here when he returns so that you can welcome him with open arms?'

'It's a matter of courtesy to let him know that I'm out for the day.'

'And you think he'd worry while he has your red-haired companion alongside?'

Caran did not bother to reply. She scribbled a note and left it in a conspicuous place in the porch. Most likely she would be home long before Paul and Julie returned from their trip.

In Brooke's shabby estate car as he drove along the coast road Caran wondered why he had invited her to accompany him, but he would never give her a straight answer even if she asked.

74

She knew that they were approaching the fishing village of Matana and somewhere nearby were some of Don Ramiro's estates.

'Can you see that old ruined castle up on the hill?' Brooke waved a hand in its direction. 'One of the places formerly owned by the Mendosas, ancestors of your friend Don Ramiro.'

She was startled by the way in which it appeared that he had read her thoughts. 'I hardly think I could be considered as a friend of Don Ramiro,' she answered. 'One drive from Granada and one dinner here doesn't exactly put me into that exclusive circle.'

'Oh?' He gave her a momentary glance of surprise. 'Is that all? You haven't made much headway, have you?'

'Some time ago you were warning me about his villainous motives,' she pointed out. 'Now you're telling me that I ought to be running after him.'

Brooke laughed loudly. 'The idea of your running after Don Ramiro is very comical indeed. All I meant was——'

'Whatever you meant isn't important,' she snapped crossly.

'Then why does a simple remark make you so indignant?' he queried in the smoothest of tones.

She realised immediately that by rising to his bait she had weakened her own position; she must learn to play it cool with Brooke when he probed into her friendships.

Now she judged it better not to reply too hastily in case she floundered still further. After a few moments she asked, 'Would you have any old cast-off clothes for Felipe, Gabriela's husband? He tries to dress respectably for his work as a waiter, but his off-duty clothes are so thin and shabby.'

He negotiated a sharp bend as the road wound downhill into Matana. 'An adroit change of subject,' he murmured. 'Well, I might find him something, I suppose, although most of the time I'm wearing my own old clothes.'

'Yes, I know—serviceable jackets and trousers when you're working up at the site, but if you had an old sweater, I think Felipe would be glad of it.'

'I'll do my best,' he promised. 'Are you giving your own delightful dresses to Gabriela?'

Caran smiled. 'She's shorter and plumper than I am, but I thought I might buy her a dress or two and some for the children in Albarosa, if I can find some way of giving them to her without offending her pride.'

He nodded. 'Well, that's a good mark you've earned. At least you've begun to understand the fierce Spanish pride that keeps many of the people struggling against circumstances that would cripple others.'

'Thank you for the compliment,' she murmured in a mock humble voice.

'Has it occurred to you why there's been so much trouble at the villas, people not wanting to work there?'

'Naturally. If they don't receive payment, they're not likely to continue putting in their labour.'

'There's more to it than that,' Brooke said decisively. 'With Spaniards, it isn't always a sheer question of money, although they like to receive what they believe they've earned. But Paul Fernwood handles everyone so badly. He has the finesse of a bulldozer. Even you do better than that.'

'I suppose you mean I have the finesse of a small lorry?'

'My goodness, you make it difficult for a man to give you even the smallest compliment!' he complained.

'Well, two compliments from you in a couple of minutes quite bowl me over!'

He had left the outskirts of the village of Matana and was now climbing away from the coast towards the lower slopes of the mountains. On either side of the road were terraced vineyards or olive groves, but away to the west the sierras were bare with a warm rose-brown tint.

'Is your irrigation site somewhere near here?' Caran asked after a few miles.

'No. It's much farther west and on the south side of the sierra,' he told her.

'Is it a long job?' she continued. 'Does it take several years?'

'That depends on the size, of course. The one I'm working on is comparatively small. Others in Spain are three times as large, according to the area of supply. Then again, this south-east part of Spain is very fertile already. It grows a tremendous amount of fruit—oranges, melons, figs, grapes. So large irrigation schemes or dams are not so necessary. It's in the interior of the country where the waterworks are needed.'

'Have you worked in other parts of Spain on similar schemes?' asked Caran.

'Several. One up in the Guadarramas, fifty or so miles from Madrid. There was good skiing not far away. Now that's something that Spain is developing. People think of Spain as sun-baked beaches, but it's also a very mountainous country with plenty of snow. All directions, too. Up in the Pyrenees where there are some of the most beautiful mountain valleys. Cantabria and, of course, right handy here, the Sierra Nevada.'

'Oh, yes, I saw the snow peaks there when I came in to Granada.'

'Do you ski?' he asked abruptly.

Caran confessed that she did not. 'Apart from Scotland, we haven't much opportunity at home and I'm afraid I've always taken my holidays in the summer so that I could go to some warm place.'

'Conventional,' he muttered. 'You should strike out more adventurously. Take holidays at different times and go to exciting places. If it's sunshine you want, there are plenty of resorts that offer that in the winter, apart from Spain. All North Africa, for instance, other parts of the Mediterranean, a whole host of places.'

'My salary was never exactly in the top bracket,' she said sharply, 'and I could remind you that if not exactly a holiday, I'm doing something different by being here in Spain all the winter.'

He gave her an unexpected beaming smile that yet held a tinge of mockery. 'And so you are. Goodness knows how you'll cope when the tourists come descending on you.'

'No doubt I shall manage,' she assured him. 'That reminds me, how are you getting on with your painting at the villa?'

'You ought to know that. If you can't tell whether my villa has been repainted or not, then it didn't need labour spent on it in the first place.'

'All I can see is the outside. I don't know what the inside's like,' she retorted.

'Same as it was last year,' he answered. 'If I'm not supplied with the paint and tools, I can't do the job, can I?'

'Not supplied with the paint?' she echoed. 'But I saw one of the workmen actually deliver it outside your porch. That was days ago.'

'Maybe,' he agreed, 'but someone, perhaps Paul or a workman, came and took it away again.'

'Some mistake. A workman must have misunderstood. All right, I'll see that you have a fresh supply tomorrow,' she declared.

'No use giving me your instructions when I'm to do the job. I've no time tomorrow. I've other work to do. If I'm taking a day off today, I must make up some of the time tomorrow.'

She was about to answer impatiently that the repainting must be done soon, but he was approaching a small town and searching for a suitable parking place.

A confused din was in progress and she could not distinguish exactly what caused it. Bellringers, certainly, but other instruments, too.

'I hope we're not too late for the main happenings,' muttered Brooke as he parked the car in a small alleyway.

She accompanied him as he hurried through the streets and now her ears received the full brunt of the noise. Men and boys ringing bells went from house to house, ostensibly to collect money. Some held guitars or metal castanets, others banged small drums, but everyone made as much clangour as possible. Brooke had a handful of small change and tossed coins into the cloth bags held out by the boys.

In the square a procession was forming outside the church and Brooke adjusted his camera.

'Can you write shorthand?' he asked Caran suddenly.

'Of course.'

'Then write down notes for me. Here's a notebook.'

So his purpose in bringing her today had not been merely to give her an outing to a place of interest. She was expected to make herself useful. Curiously, his peremptory command did not provoke her to an angry response. In spite of herself she accepted the task with pleasure, slightly gratified to be helping him.

He began dictating quietly the scene as it happened, describing the church dignitaries in their gold or purple robes, the boys in long white trousers and short red jackets; then came the centrepiece of the procession. To Caran it looked like a giant bun in the form of a garland, and was borne on a white velvet-covered platform.

'It's called the *Rosca*, that outsize bun or cake,' explained Brooke. 'The women of the village make it, each one contributes part of the ingredients, flour, eggs, sugar, so on, and we shall see it taken into the church to be blessed and laid at the feet of the patron image.'

In listening to his explanation she had forgotten to write her shorthand notes until he said impatiently, 'Go on, write it down, or we shall both forget.'

Caran could not imagine that she would easily forget the occasion, but she realised that Brooke had seen many of these local fiestas and might easily confuse one with another.

Together they watched the brief ceremony in the crowded church where the priest blessed the huge garland, a structure some four feet tall, a beautiful shiny brown sculpture of entwined leaves and flowers. Caran wondered where such a remarkable item of cookery could be baked, but supposed that a local baker had an adequate oven.

Again the *Rosca* was carefully hoisted on to its white velvet plinth and carried out of the church to the square. At this point Brooke climbed some steps on the opposite side and took more photographs. Caran stayed close beside him all the time, fearing that if she lost sight of him he would afterwards scold her for not being available as his secretary.

'Where do they take the bun now?' she asked him as the procession moved away.

'Just around the main streets and back again.' He now led the way through the side street so that they could see the small procession from another point. 'Nothing more exciting there, I think. We'll wait for them to return to the square.'

In the square Brooke found a place on some steps where they could wait. Already a large number of women in long black dresses, red and white embroidered jackets and colourful headscarves had gathered in the centre of the square.

'Now what happens?' queried Caran.

'Those who wait patiently generally manage to find out,' he teased her.

'Not always. You might be waiting in the wrong place or at the wrong time and the exciting experience bypass you completely.'

He turned to glance at her. 'A penetrating snippet of philosophy! I must remember that. It could affect my whole future life.'

In her turn Caran gave him a derisive glance. 'Am I supposed to be taking down your remarks or are these exchanges strictly off the cuff?'

But now with a great clamour of bells, tambourines, guitars and drums, the procession entered the square and halted in the centre. The crowd of women waited while two trestle tables were erected, covered with white cloths and the *Rosca* carefully placed down. The blue and white ribbon streamers were removed and each woman cut a small piece of the bun. When all the women moved away, this was the signal for a great rush of men, women and children to secure fragments of what was left.

Brooke was standing up, filming the ceremony with his ciné-camera. 'Those who are lucky enough to get pieces,' he told Caran, 'either keep them as lucky charms or else give them to their animals to ward off disease.'

She scribbled some hurried notes in her book, although she knew she was not likely to forget any single detail of today's scenes.

When the crowds had dispersed to the boom and blare of drums and musical instruments, Brooke suggested that he would take her to lunch at a small inn a couple of miles away. 'All the places here will be far too crowded today.'

He manoeuvred his car through the narrow streets and out on to a winding road farther into the mountains. At the inn the proprietor welcomed Brooke enthusiastically, greeting him as an old friend who had stayed away too long, but Caran was treated with an enquiring glance.

She was amused because she imagined that as Brooke was so well known here, he had probably been accompanied on previous occasions by other girls and the proprietor was curious about this new acquaintance, especially as Brooke had introduced her as an English *señorita*. Caran remembered Paul's derisive insinuations that Brooke's absences from the villa were accounted for by his dallying with girls of the neighbourhood.

During the meal Caran checked her notes with Brooke.

'I'm glad to find you can read your shorthand,' he said. 'I must take you to other places as my amanuensis.'

She was about to retort that she would let him know her terms, but that would sound like money-grubbing and finance was far from her thoughts today, for in spite of Brooke's occasional digs, she found she was thoroughly enjoying herself in his company.

At the end of the meal a young girl about seventeen or eighteen served coffee, but when she saw Brooke she set down the tray with a clatter.

'*Buenas tardes*, Angelina,' Brooke greeted the girl, who blushed furiously, muttered a greeting in return and promptly fled to the door, but she could not resist a backward look that took in Caran. Then she gave Brooke a nervous smile and vanished.

'Is she the proprietor's daughter?' queried Caran in a matter-of-fact voice.

'His niece.' Brooke laughed quietly as though remembering past pleasures. 'She's not always so shy.'

'She probably prefers you to be unencumbered with English companions,' commented Caran, pouring the coffee.

When they left the inn, Caran noticed that Angelina sidled round a door in the passage and would have dodged back again, but Brooke took her wrist and held her prisoner.

Caran smiled at the girl and walked slowly towards Brooke's car, leaving the pair to chat for a moment without her presence, but Brooke followed her, still holding Angelina's hand.

'This is Angelina,' he introduced her to Caran, then turned to the Spanish girl. 'The English *señorita* is Miss Ingram.'

The two girls exchanged acknowledgments and smiles.

'Angelina tells me she's betrothed,' Brooke explained. 'To some mountain brigand or other.'

Caran congratulated the girl in Spanish and Angelina was clearly delighted that an English girl could speak a foreign tongue. Her confidence restored, she babbled happily about her future husband who owned vineyards already and would soon own many more so that one day he would be rich.

Then she stopped suddenly and asked, 'You also are now betrothed?' Her glance took in both Brooke and Caran.

Brooke smiled and seemed in no hurry to refute this suggestion, but Caran said quickly, 'Oh, no, indeed. That is not so.'

Brooke gave a slight shrug. 'I could speak for myself, of course, but you understand, Angelina, that Señorita Ingram might have a fiancé in England.'

Caran smiled, aware that her face must be fiery. She gave Angelina a warm *'Adios'* and went towards Brooke's car.

He joined her after a few moments and drove in silence for a mile or two. Then he asked suddenly, 'Why are you annoyed? Because I hinted you might have a man you left behind you in England?'

'No. I'm not annoyed,' she said smoothly.

Brooke laughed. 'How well you parry questions you don't want to answer! All right, I shan't pester you or insist on knowing. Of course, if you're going to be here for a really long time, he'd be right in jilting you.'

'M'm, that could be,' she agreed. She was not going to satisfy his curiosity. After all, if she dared to ask him if he were engaged or had left a hopeful girl behind him in England or elsewhere, he would probably give her a sharp answer or none at all.

A turn of the mountain road brought a wide panorama into view, the long sweeping plain dotted with one town and several villages, the distant strip of sea, and on the other side the mass of grey mountains sharply etched against the setting sun. Brooke stopped the car so that Caran could enjoy the scene. He lit a thin cigar and stepped out, opening the door her side so that she, too, could alight.

'How lonely it is up here,' she said. 'We haven't passed another car for miles.'

'Pleasant change to have so little traffic, I should think, from reports I read of the shocking jams at home. Parts of the Continent are just as bad. Are you afraid of lonely places?'

Leaning against the side of the car she stared at the distant view. 'Not in the least—unless we're in danger of being attacked by those mountain brigands you spoke of to Angelina.'

'Unlikely, I'd say.' He pointed away to the right. 'I don't know whether you can see it, but down there is Don Ramiro's very handsome villa.'

She could faintly glimpse a white villa partly hidden by trees.

'Have you been there?' she queried.

He grunted. 'I'm not at all in the right circle for an aristocrat like Don Ramiro to invite me there.'

'I suppose he uses that villa only in the summer?'

'He opens it up occasionally, I believe, but most of the time he lives in Almeria in a smallish ducal palace, his ancestral home. Now that's a handsome piece of architecture.' He broke off to smile at her. 'No, I haven't been inside there, either, but the outside is charming. Have you visited Almeria yet?'

'Well, no, I haven't really had time,' admitted Caran.

'You'll have to make time for these occasions before the summer or else you'll be too busy then.'

Even as they watched, the sun dropped abruptly behind the shoulder of a mountain, the pink glow faded from the plain and a chilly wind sprang up.

When Brooke had finished his cigar, they re-entered the car and he drove through the dusk along the winding roads. They came to a small town where they stopped at a café. Caran chose coffee with Tía Maria, for the night air was chilly, but Brooke drank only a small brandy.

'Would you like to have dinner at Matana?' he asked. 'Good fish restaurants there.'

'Yes, I'd like that,' agreed Caran. Matana was the fishing village along the coast only a few miles from Albarosa, so that meant she would not be too late home. But she had reckoned without Brooke's idea of dinner-time and without realising exactly where she was now. It was nearly nine o'clock when they reached Matana and although she was by now accustomed to Spanish meal-times and nine o'clock was the usual hour, she felt apprehensive about Paul not finding her at the villas when he returned. But of this she said nothing to Brooke. He would only jeer and taunt her with trying to please Paul at all costs.

The restaurant to which Brooke eventually took her was near the harbour. It was dim, with only small green lanterns on the walls, and the furniture was all black wood. But the food was a revelation to Caran. Brooke ordered the special *zarzuela* for which Matana was famous—a mixed fish dish including mussels, prawns, crayfish and whiting and several other varieties unknown to Caran. She enjoyed every succulent mouthful, but when Brooke suggested *solomillo* to follow, she objected that she couldn't possibly eat one of these thick steaks, but would content herself with fruit and cheese.

It was very late when at last Brooke drove home and Caran saw that Julie was already in the bedroom.

'Hallo, pet! We wondered where you were. Had a good day?'

'Very good indeed,' replied Caran.

'Where did you go?'

'Oh, to this little village where the fiesta was held today, then out through the mountains and back to Matana.'

'This Brooke Eldridge must be fascinating.'

Something in Julie's tone made Caran look across the room at her.

'Fascinating? Oh, I wouldn't say that,' replied Caran coolly. 'He's interesting, but then he's lived here in Spain quite some time. He knows the district.'

Julie fluttered the pages of a fashion magazine.

Caran asked, 'And you? Did you have a good day with Paul?'

The magazine was flung on the floor. 'No, I didn't. He's getting rather too amorous for my liking,' declared Julie.

'Well, I suppose that's because you're here on holiday and he thinks he has to show you the sights and take you around to places.' Caran was mildly surprised at Julie's objection.

'I'm aware of that and of course I'm pleased to be taken here and there for a spot of gaiety, but he needn't make himself such a nuisance.'

Caran laughed. 'Oh, come off it, Julie! With your expertise you know just how to fend off any man's unwelcome attentions. I don't remember that you've ever made these objections over any other man so far. What's wrong with Paul?'

Julie made a grimace. She was sitting up in bed, a cream lace negligée around her shoulders, her red-gold hair brushed and shining. She hugged her knees under the bedclothes. 'Nothing much is wrong with Paul. I don't dislike him.'

'He's rather taken with you,' remarked Caran, as she creamed her face. 'He wanted to know if you were staying here over Christmas.'

'Yes, he asked me this morning and, like a fool, I said yes, I was.'

'Why like a fool? Christmas here in Spain can be very interesting, as well as all the first week in January. You're welcome to stay, as far as I'm concerned.'

Julie smiled in that curious lop-sided way she affected sometimes. 'Paul is doing his best to persuade me to stay on indefinitely, not only just for Christmas and New Year.'

'Indefinitely?' echoed Caran, more alert. 'But your job— you couldn't expect——'

'Leave me to worry about my job,' interrupted Julie with determined coolness. 'I can go back to that any time. The truth is, Caran, my pet, I'm tired of the humdrum life I've been leading, just as you were. I need a change, not for a couple of weeks or so, but for quite a few months, so I might stay here with you.'

'And how will you deal with Paul? If you're bored with

him already, you won't like the situation here.'

'I think I can take care of that,' Julie assured the other. 'Actually, we might find each other quite useful, Paul and I. He's a very astute business man and today he was telling me all his plans for the development of this place.'

'Oh, I expect he wants to increase the number of villas. He's spoken to me about that.'

'Rather more than a few villas. Paul means to make Albarosa into the newest, most fashionable resort along this part of the coast. He says it's just sitting here waiting for someone like him to come along and really start things sizzling.'

Caran stared at her friend. 'How does he propose to develop the place?'

Julie turned her lovely brown eyes on Caran. 'But, darling, surely you must know more about Paul's plans than I do. Hasn't he confided in you?'

Caran shook her head.

'I'm surprised,' commented Julie. 'I should have thought that you were completely in his confidence. Well, he wants to put up a couple of decent hotels for a start.'

'Where?'

'Oh, somewhere near here. On the beach anyway. That's what people come for. But the hotels will have their own swimming pools, of course. An elegant little night-club or two, dancing—all the usual trimmings that drag a sleepy little town into the modern trend.'

Caran was silent for a few moments. Then she burst out, 'Why can't he leave Albarosa alone? These villas are just right for visitors who want to get away from it all. If people want to go to Torremolinos or the Costa Brava, that's where they go. They come here for peace and quietness, not up-ended matchbox hotels and noisy bars and smoke-filled night-clubs.'

'Really, Caran!' Julie's eyebrows arched upwards. 'What's so upsetting about a modern holiday project? You're not frightened of losing your job, are you? Good heavens, there'll be the pick of some very plummy posts for you and me if we want them.'

'Most likely. But I'm not sure that I want any part in destroying the natural charm of this place. Albarosa is unspoilt and I like it that way.' She thumped her pillows as though she were pummelling an enemy. Paul, perhaps?

Julie took her cue and switched out the lights. 'Perhaps you've an idea that your friend Brooke might not like any new development and go elsewhere?'

'What he does and where he goes is his affair,' replied Caran. 'He's not here permanently anyway. When his irrigation job is finished, he'll probably go off to another.'

'Oh, I see,' said Julie in her creamiest voice. 'In that case I must make his acquaintance speedily before he flits off.'

Caran did not answer. She was too upset by this unexpected news of Paul's plans for the ruin of Albarosa to care much about Julie's campaign to become friendly with Brooke. Brooke must look after himself. If he became too involved with Julie that would be his responsibility.

CHAPTER FIVE

Caran tackled Paul at the earliest opportunity, the following morning. She began quietly enough by saying, 'I hear from Julie that you've quite ambitious plans in mind for the development of Albarosa.'

'That's right,' he agreed. His plump face became animated. 'Hotels, a row of shops perhaps, a little de luxe resort on its own with the town of Albarosa up on the hill. The odd thing is that no one has started already to modernise the place.'

'Modernising nowadays usually means changing the whole character of the place. I thought all you wanted to do was build a few more villas.'

Paul frowned. 'Not profitable enough. Even if they were absolutely full all the year round, what do they hold? A mere handful of people. On the same amount of space we could build a smart hotel, four or five storeys, say, and we'd have a couple of hundred rooms at the least.'

'Then Albarosa will be like any other resort, not only in Spain, but all over the Continent. Conventional hotels, swimming pools, everything for the package-tourists.'

'But that's what people want!' declared Paul angrily. 'And don't despise package-tourists. They're the life-blood of the holiday industry. They come by the plane-load, and what they want is a modern hotel down by the beach where they can swim when they choose, loll about in the sun, join up with holiday acquaintances for a drink or two in the evening. You have to remember that Spain has the climate for that kind of holiday and at home in England we haven't—or at least it's not reliable enough. You can freeze sometimes in August.'

'I understand all that, but why must every spot on the coast have to be the same? Wouldn't it be an advantage to advertise that Albarosa is different?'

Paul shrugged. 'Not really.'

'You mean there isn't enough profit in it?' She spoke mildly enough, but Paul sensed the underlying scorn in her voice.

'Look, Caran, I don't know why you're so opposed to the scheme. You're not worried about losing your job, are you?'

He was echoing Julie's view that there would be any amount of new jobs for those who wanted them. 'No, that's the last thing that worries me,' she said evenly. She was aware that he was reminding her that she was a paid employee. 'But whatever my own views might be, I couldn't object to any plans you have, could I? The decisions don't rest with me.'

'That's true,' he conceded. 'All the same, I'd like to feel that you were on my side in all that we're trying to do.'

'I think you can always rely on me to carry out your instructions.'

He laughed and placed a hand on her shoulder. 'Oh, come, Caran, I want something more than that. It will depress me to feel that all our future plans will only meet with your disapproval.'

She smiled. 'I wouldn't put it so sweeping as that. I suppose it's inevitable. No place as unspoilt as Albarosa can stay the same way indefinitely.'

'Exactly. It must either move forward or decay. Now come into my villa and I can show you some of our plans.'

There was no alternative but to follow him and perhaps it was better for her to know as much as possible about the future. Or at least as much as Paul was willing to tell her.

On the table in his living room he took out a bundle of maps and architects' plans. 'Now here are our five villas and over there the two still being built.' He pointed to their position on the map. 'Now the most attractive way to develop would be to the north along this inlet.'

'Where the two new villas are?' she queried.

'Yes, more or less.'

Caran's hopes rose. A new hotel on that site would not be conspicuous, for the sloping ground would hide most of it except from the sea.

'But the big snag is the land. My aunt doesn't really own the land on which our villas are built. She has a concession for ten years, after which it could be renewed, but only at the discretion of the owner.'

'Something like a lease?'

Paul nodded. 'Something like that, but the property laws here are slightly different from those at home. That's one of the many reasons why I'm here. I have to negotiate with the owner not only of our piece, but the site along the spit of shore which juts out.'

'And is that difficult?'

'Almost impossible, so far. You see, there's a rival concern that also wants to build hotels right in this same place.'

'Poor Albarosa!' she murmured gently. 'Between these various industrial factions, this little town's fate is sealed.'

'But think what prosperity all this will bring to the town! Shops and cafés and all kinds of small tradesmen will benefit.'

'Yes, I know they will.' Caran had a sudden vision of Felipe, Gabriela's husband. Would more prosperity enable him to get a better job and house his family more adequately?

Paul's attention was again on the drawings. 'This plot of land is the one we want. You see what a wonderful situation it is? By building the first hotel on the north side of the jutting strip, we could then in due course build another or extend the first across the neck of the peninsula and the customers would have the choice of two beaches. M'm, that wouldn't be a bad name for such a hotel. What's the Spanish for Peninsula?'

'Peninsula,' Caran told him with a laugh.

'Yes, that sounds good. Hotel Peninsula. Well, we're running way ahead. First thing is to obtain the land.'

'Have you good hopes of succeeding?' she asked.

'Not really, but if we can't get exactly what we want, we might find other ways of compromising.'

'Don Ramiro is an influential man around these parts. Couldn't he help?'

Paul's head shot up with a jerk. 'Don Ramiro? You're

joking!' He gave her a long, appraising stare. Then he said thoughtfully, 'He might be able to help us in some way. I've an idea. I'll try to fix a visit to him within the next few days and I'll take you and Julie along with me. How about that?'

'In Almeria?' she queried.

'Yes. His villa here is shut.'

Caran became slightly uneasy. She wished now that she had not mentioned Don Ramiro. By suggesting that he could help Paul in some way, she had aligned herself with Paul and his projects, which had been far from her intention.

'What am I expected to do on this visit?' she asked.

'Do? Nothing at all. It's merely a social visit.'

She discounted that. She guessed that Paul wanted to take both girls along to make it look like a social visit, but, if opportunity offered, he would persuade Don Ramiro to engage in a business discussion.

Paul rolled up his drawings and sketches and for a few minutes he and Caran discussed other details in connection with the villas. As she turned to leave he asked, 'Where did you go yesterday?'

'Brooke took me to a village in the mountains for a special fiesta,' she answered casually.

'Brooke? Oh, you mean Eldridge.' Paul smiled. 'Yes, I'd forgotten he was also known here as Señor Brooke.'

Caran felt her face redden. 'You'd already gone out or I'd have asked your permission for the day off, of course,' she said.

He waved his hand to brush away such a ludicrous idea. 'You're free to go out when you choose.'

'Thank you,' she muttered, and hurried out of the villa.

She wondered sometimes how to take Paul. His attitudes were changeable and his remarks were not always to be taken at their face value. Did he now also mean that she was free to go out with whom she chose? She had taken that for granted, of course, within reason, but since Julie's appearance, Paul had spent much of his time taking Julie out and about. Caran saw no reason why she should refuse invitations because they did not come from Paul.

It occurred now to her that if Paul was trying to arrange a visit to Don Ramiro, she ought to find out how matters stood with Gabriela and Felipe. She might find an opportunity of jogging his memory about helping them to find new accommodation.

She went to the Villa Cristal and was surprised that none of the children was playing outside. The outer door was firmly shut. She knocked, but no sound came from within. Then she noticed the large key hanging on a nail in the porch. She had not thought to bring her own bunch.

Inside, the villa was clean and tidy. No sign of litter anywhere, the bedding was neatly folded on each bed, the flower vases had been washed and polished.

Caran stood in the living room astonished. Idly she ran a finger over the polished dining table and there was no mark of dust. In the kitchen a tap dripped and she made a mental note to have a new washer fixed; the refrigerator had been switched off and the door left ajar.

Where had Gabriela and her family gone? And when? Caran could only suppose that they had moved out yesterday when she was out for the day. Surely otherwise, Gabriela would have come and told Caran that she had found accommodation.

Caran returned to her own villa for the inventory. She had no doubts about Gabriela's honesty, but for the sake of good business management, she must check that all the furniture and equipment remained in the Villa Cristal. Then there would be no misunderstanding or confusion if queries arose and Gabriela and Felipe could not be blamed for shortages or damage.

Everything was intact and in order, she found. Indeed, there was one item that did not appear on her inventory, a small rag doll lying on a bedroom window-sill. She picked it up, wondering to which of the smaller children it had belonged.

There was no point in asking Brooke for information where Gabriela had gone. He was sure to be away on the irrigation site, for he had to make up for yesterday's outing, so he had told her. But there were two other people who would surely know, Benita and Felipe.

First she must tell Paul that the villa was free.

'And about time, too,' he said. 'I wasn't going to let them have much more rope. I told them a week ago that it was their last chance and if they didn't get out, I'd have them put out—by the police if necessary.'

'Oh, Paul! It wasn't necessary to threaten them like that!' Caran's tone was one of shocked surprise. 'They were doing their best.'

'They had no right to occupy the villa in the first place,' he retorted. 'It was rather too easy, with that old biddy, the mother, having the keys and being able to do as she liked during the winter.'

Caran turned away. 'They were desperate,' she murmured.

'Desperate they might be—probably still are, but it's not our pigeon. We're not in business to rescue homeless Spanish families, however deserving.' After a pause he moved towards her and thrust an arm around her shoulders. 'Cheer up, Caran. There's no need for you to be so anxious about them. Let's both be glad they've gone without any unpleasantness.' He planted a swift kiss on her cheek, and at that moment Julie came through the porch and into the living room.

'Oh, sorry! Have I interrupted something?' she enquired. 'I'll disappear if you want to continue the touching little scene.'

Caran immediately broke away from Paul's grasp. 'You're welcome to stay,' she told Julie with a smile. 'Paul and I occasionally have our unbusinesslike moments.' She was astounded to hear her own voice saying these unexpected words. What had possessed her to pretend that her relationship with Paul was not always on a purely business level?

'I went along to the end villa where this fascinating irrigation man lives,' Julie said, flopping into an armchair, 'but his place is all shut up. What's happened?'

Caran smiled. 'Remember that he works sometimes. He's probably up in the hills somewhere, paddling about among his waterways. Did you want specially to see him?'

Before she answered Julie cast an upward glance at Paul,

then lowered her long lashes. 'I thought he might be amusing to talk to. With you two engrossed in your business affairs all the time, nothing very exciting seems to be going on.'

Julie's heavy emphasis on the words 'business affairs' did not escape Caran's notice, but it was better not to argue about that with Paul still in the room. Instead she pointed out, 'You and Paul were out gadding yesterday, and so was I, come to that.' Caran smiled disarmingly. 'We have to work part of the time—same as Brooke.'

Paul fidgeted with some of the papers on his dining table. Since Julie's entrance he had appeared ill at ease. Now he said, 'I'll go out and see how the men are getting on with the painting. Now that the squatters have gone, we can make a start on that villa soon.'

As soon as he was clear of the porch, Julie let out a long peal of laughter. 'Oh, poor Paul!' she exclaimed when she could speak. 'Went off like a scalded cat! Just as though I care if he makes a few passes at you, dear Caran, on the side.'

Caran felt the swift colour mount into her face. 'I don't suppose you do, but then I'm not concerned if he flirts with you either. I'm not at all enamoured of him.'

'That's a comfort to us all.' Julie rose from the armchair. 'I shouldn't like to see you get in too deep with him. He's a philanderer if ever I saw one, but at the same time he could be quite useful.'

'You mean in giving us well-paid and exciting jobs?'

Julie made a small grimace. 'Jobs come into it, of course, but I wasn't thinking so much of work.'

Caran laughed. 'I'll bet you weren't! You and real work always prefer to pass by on the other side of the street.'

Julie's head went up. 'I deny that. I've worked hard in my time. Acting and modelling are strenuous, and as for that year I spent in journalism, I was simply run off my feet.'

Caran grinned. 'That year in journalism amounted to about three weeks. You thought you were going to interview the famous and potter about at Ascot and the paper sent you to cover obscure weddings and funerals.'

It was true that Julie had experimented with a variety of occupations. After the course at drama school she had failed to secure anything but a walk-on part in a play that closed after a fortnight. A spell of modelling for a fashion house was followed by a short stint on a weekly paper. After that she drifted into free-lancing for various photographers, demonstrating fashions or knitting patterns, walking on springy carpets or basking in the warmth of efficient central heating.

Caran's opinion was that in this last category of jobs, Julie had achieved her greatest success. Her shining red-gold hair, brown eyes and dazzling smile were all entirely photogenic and her personality came over on the printed pages of magazines.

Beside Julie, Caran knew herself to be diminished. When they had shared a flat their jobs had divided them during the day, they met sometimes for an evening meal when Julie had no man to take her out to dinner. Breakfast was a rush with one eye always on the clock.

But now with Julie here all day unless she was out with Paul, Caran was aware that her own personality, her lively spirit, her zest in helping to manage the villas was slowly evaporating, leaving her a negative shadow in the background.

Caran told herself that she must snap out of such self-deprecatory attitudes and recover her own individuality. Julie was obviously bored for the time being with Paul and needed a new stimulus of masculine gender. Let her tackle Brooke, then, and if he proved a harder nut to crack than Julie expected, then perhaps that would keep her pleasantly occupied all the longer.

With these thoughts running through her mind, Caran picked up her inventory lists and moved towards the porch of Paul's villa.

'I must go back to Joyosa,' she said. 'My day out yesterday has left me with plenty to do. I've also Brooke's notes to type out for him when I have time.'

'Notes? What notes would they be?' Julie was instantly alerted.

'Oh, just some jottings about the fiesta generally,' Caran

answered casually. She realised that she had been slightly indiscreet.

'Why does he want notes about it?' queried Julie. 'Does he write for the papers or something?'

'Nothing like that, I think. He's been in various parts of Spain on irrigation schemes and I suppose he likes to keep some sort of record.'

Caran escaped before Julie could ask any more questions.

The Villa Joyosa was in its usual state of untidiness, with Julie's possessions strewn about and as Caran collected shoes from under a chair and replaced Julie's dresses in the wardrobe, it occurred to her that Julie could make herself more useful. At the present time most of the domestic work fell upon Caran, who had to try to keep the villas, her own and Paul's, clean. In addition, she usually prepared lunch for the three when they were all at home. So far, no maids had been engaged, but that was a point on which she must soon approach Paul.

'Yes, I've been thinking about that,' Paul agreed, when she mentioned the subject. 'We must find some suitable girls in the town. There ought to be plenty. What about that girl who was here last year? Benita, I think her name was.'

'I told you she was working in a shop in the town,' returned Caran.

'We'll see if we can get her back again. A pretty little piece, if I remember.' Into Paul's eyes came a reminiscent glow.

'I'll ask her,' promised Caran.

She was anxious to see Benita on her own account, for she wanted to know where Gabriela and her family had gone and if they were comfortably accommodated.

She called at the shack where Manuela and Benita lived, but the girl was apparently not in a very talkative mood. She was busy sewing the hem of a new flamenco dress, one with a red satin bodice and black lace flounces edged with red.

'I came because I wanted to know what your sister and her family had found a comfortable place to live,' explained Caran, after her first enquiries had met with silence or a muttered '*Si*' or '*No*'.

96

'She is comfortable,' asserted Benita.

'Is it possible for me to see them? Where do they live now?'

Benita lifted an alarmed face. 'Not possible. Gabriela would not like that.'

Caran shrugged. There was no point in pursuing that tack.

'How would you like to come back to the villas and work instead of in the shop?' she asked. 'We could offer you good wages and this time I promise that you will be paid properly every week without fail. If she's not too far away, perhaps your sister could also help.'

Benita shook her head. 'No,' she said at last. 'I do not wish to work in the villas.'

'Why? You were happy enough last year, weren't you? Oh, I know you had too much to do, but we could avoid that this year. We will take on enough maids for all the villas.'

Benita's refusal was even more vehement.

'If the English *señor* persuades you to come, would you agree?' asked Caran.

She was unprepared for the storm of hostility that her innocuous question aroused.

Benita flung aside the dress and jumped to her feet. 'I will not come for the English *señor*! I do not like him.'

Caran stared at the Spanish girl. 'But I thought you liked him quite well—unless you've quarrelled with him. Why, only the other day he was taking your photograph in your other flamenco dress.'

A wave of relief broke over Benita's features. 'Oh, yes, the Señor Brooke. Yes, he is kind. But the other English *señor*, the one called Pablo—him I do not like.'

'I see.' Caran accepted the position. If the girl disliked Paul, there was nothing to be done.

'Not even the Señor Brooke would wish me to work in the villas again after——' Benita broke off abruptly.

Caran smiled encouragingly, but did not press the girl for further information. Paul had remembered Benita, so it was not difficult to guess that at some time last year he had flirted rather too heavily with this attractive Spanish girl.

'Then if you know other girls in Albarosa who would be willing to come to us, would you let me know?'

Benita's full rich mouth became a thin red line. '*Señorita*, you have been kind to my family and for this I would like to help you, but if the Señor Pablo is to stay here for a long time, then the girls will not come.'

'I'm sorry about that,' was all that Caran could say at this moment. The villas apparently had a bad reputation with the girls of Albarosa.

'Then you see I have my dancing,' continued Benita in a happier tone. 'If I were a maid in a villa, I could not also be dancing in the evenings.'

'We could arrange that for you, no doubt,' offered Caran, 'but anyway, think it over and if you change your mind, come and tell me.'

Benita smiled, a slow, sad smile that told Caran that there was not the slightest possibility that the girl would change her mind.

Benita picked up the flamenco dress again and made a courteous little gesture towards Caran. 'You will permit me to continue with the sewing?'

'Of course. It's a handsome dress. A new one?'

Benita's eyes softened as she smiled. 'Yes. The Señor Brooke bought it for me. But last night at the café I tore one of the flounces, so I must repair it.'

'I see. *Adios*, Benita.'

Caran was thoughtful on her way back to her villa. So Benita apparently detested Paul because he had probably pawed her once too often and Brooke bought her new flamenco dresses. An interesting situation, she reflected. Was Brooke also responsible for finding accommodation for Gabriela? She now suspected that he had invited her to the fiesta so that she should not be on the spot when Gabriela and her family moved out. But why couldn't he have told her?

The next evening Paul took both Julie and Caran to dinner at the Marroqui restaurant in Albarosa, the one to which Don Ramiro had first taken her and where Benita usually danced.

The evening could scarcely be called a success. Paul over-played his hand by devoting most of his attention to Caran and almost ignoring Julie. Possibly he was trying to make Julie jealous, but Caran could have told him that this was not the method.

After Benita's performance Paul beckoned to the girl, in-viting her to join him at the table, but she smiled graciously and with a provocative twirl of her skirts disappeared through a door at the side of the dais on which the musicians played.

'Surely you don't have to invite tenth-rate flamenco dancers to join us,' complained Julie, moodily gazing into her wineglass.

'She isn't only a dancer,' put in Caran quickly. 'She lives near the villas and I've been trying to persuade her to work for us as a maid.'

'She seemed all right last year,' murmured Paul.

Julie immediately smiled. 'Oh, last year! All is now clear. She had enough of you, Paul. Somewhere you slipped up and offended her. Now she won't come when you whistle to her.'

Paul flushed a little uneasily. Then he glanced from Julie to Caran and back again. 'I'm not worrying much about a Spanish dancing girl when I've you two to keep me com-pany.'

'You're not really very expert at driving tandem,' was Julie's opinion.

Caran was relieved when they were all home again. Julie's presence had created undue tensions in a situation that had started as a simple dinner for three. Next time she would insist that Paul took Julie alone. Then they could wrangle as they pleased.

Paul went off to Almeria early next morning before Julie was up.

'What a meanie!' Julie exclaimed when Caran told her. 'Not even asking me if I wanted to go with him.'

'Did you want very much to go with him? The other day you were bored by his company.'

'I'm just as bored here and at least I could have done some

shopping in Almeria,' retorted Julie.

'Then suppose you cook the lunch for us both while I run around the villas and see what's going on,' suggested Caran.

'Oh, no, indeed. I'll come with you on your inspection tour and see if this elusive Mr. Eldridge has yet returned from playing with his dams and canals or whatever they are.'

'In that case, you'll get fruit and cheese for lunch,' threatened Caran. 'Nothing else.'

'Suits me.' Julie laughed. 'We ought not to be doing these things for ourselves anyway. What are maids for?'

Caran turned to face her friend. 'All right. Then if you're so bored, go up into the town and see if you can obtain a maid or two. You've already said that Paul wants you to take on public relations work for the villas. Now's your chance to try your hand at the job. I'll give you a note of what we can pay and the number of hours they're expected to work.'

Julie gasped with astonishment, tinged with admiration.

'Caran! I'd no idea you were such a good business woman. Yes, I'll do as you say. I'll have lunch somewhere in the town, so don't wait for me.'

'Huh! I shall eat my melon and cheese whenever it suits me.' Caran gave Julie an affectionate push. 'Now get out from under my feet, there's a pet.'

Julie laughed again. 'Oh, Caran darling, that's overdoing it. Just because I said you were a good little business woman, you're imagining yourself a high-powered director of the company.'

Caran grinned but said nothing as she went out through the gardens on her way to check up the painting and decorating.

About the middle of the morning Brooke appeared. He came along the shore path towards his own villa and Caran noticed how tired he looked. His face was almost grey, he had two days' stubble on his chin and his hair was caked with mud.

'Hallo,' he greeted her, yawning.

'*Buenos dias,*' she answered. 'You look as if you've been up all night.'

'All of two nights,' he told her.

'Trouble at the irrigation works?'

'More than trouble. Nearly a catastrophe. Up in the sierra where the dam straddles across the valley, a new road is also being built. Part of the concrete work gave way and a few thousand tons of rubble cascaded down into the valley.'

'Oh, that was bad luck. Anyone hurt?'

'Fortunately, no. Or at least no one seriously damaged. One man clambered down to look for his tools and managed to hurt his leg. It was lucky there wasn't much water in the valley or we'd have been in a worse mess. As it is, it will take several weeks to clear up.'

'I expect you want a bath and some sleep,' she suggested. 'Can I get you a meal or anything?'

He rubbed his mud-stained hands through his equally muddy hair. The smile he gave her was unexpectedly amiable, almost tender. 'Thoughtful little soul, aren't you?' His tone of voice held the usual derision, whatever the smile might have conveyed.

'All I wanted was to help,' she grumbled.

'And so you shall. Give me half an hour or so to bathe and shave and change out of these horrible clothes and we'll go and lunch together at El Catalan in the town. I could do with a good solid meal—no offence to your cooking, I hope.'

'None,' she agreed, with a laugh. 'But aren't you tired?'

'Too tired to sleep until I've eaten.'

'All right. I'll be ready.' She watched him go towards his Villa Zafiro, saw how his shoulders drooped and his feet dragged along the path. She should probably have tried to insist on his going to bed at once after he had washed, but that would have been useless. If he was determined to lunch in the town she could at least see that he came home again promptly and took a long rest in the afternoon.

At the same time if they went to El Catalan, she might have a chance to ask Felipe where he was living now. She had not had an opportunity of telling Brooke about Gabriela's move, but in his rackety old estate car on the way up to the town, she told him of her surprise and the fact that she couldn't get any further news from Benita.

'So at last your friend Don Ramiro has done something for them. Or was it Paul?'

'It certainly wasn't Paul,' she answered. 'He was as surprised as the rest of us.'

'But darned glad that someone else had done the dirty work for him?'

'For a man who's nearly falling asleep over the wheel, you're surprisingly smart, but we'll let that pass. Paul was glad that he hadn't to undertake such an unpleasant task.'

'Rubbish! He'd have relished it. The wonder is that he didn't bundle the family out neck and crop long before this. Was that your doing, Caran?'

'No, I don't think so. He knew I was sympathetic to them, of course. Where have they gone?'

'How should I know? Maybe Don Ramiro has found them an excellent apartment at a nominal rent.'

Was Brooke stalling or was he really as ignorant as he pretended?

'By the way, on my way down this morning I passed your glamorous friend—what's her name—Julie. I'd have given her a lift but for the fact that she was going in the opposite direction. I didn't realise she was the kind of girl who would walk anywhere.'

'She prefers to ride, certainly, but she was going into Albarosa to try to find some maids for us. Benita won't work for the villas, I understand.'

'Too true. Not while Don Juan is knocking around. If he wants to keep maids, he should learn to keep his hands in his pockets.'

Caran did not choose to continue this conversation. While she and Julie might compare notes about Paul, it was not discreet that she should discuss her employer's nephew with a man like Brooke.

At El Catalan there was no sign of Felipe. 'Doesn't he work here now?' asked Caran when Brooke had given the order.

'Don't know. He may have taken the day off. Oh, yes, I've sorted out a couple of garments for him. You said he needed something warm.'

'Why, yes. Thank you, Brooke. But how shall I be able to give them to him?'

'Benita will pass them on.'

Benita. How fond was Brooke of that pretty Spanish dancer? Not that it mattered to Caran, of course. She supposed that many men in Brooke's position, working in a foreign country apart from all their own friends and acquaintances, might indulge in an affair or two with a girl on the spot. Leaving out Benita, there had been that girl at the mountain inn, Angelina, who had blushed at the sight of Brooke. Was she another to whom he had made transient love and who now took refuge in telling him that she was betrothed? Her engagement might be quite true, but the girl also had her pride and probably would not allow Brooke to believe that she was desolate on his account.

No doubt a number of English girls had stayed at the villas, but, if Brooke had made their acquaintance, a holiday fortnight or three weeks was insufficient for anything more than an ephemeral episode.

'You're remarkably silent,' Brooke observed now across the table. 'Is it a very knotty problem?'

'Sorry,' she apologised hastily. 'No, not a problem at all. I was only day-dreaming.'

'I could see that,' he answered crisply. 'You were frowning horribly. A few night-dreams in addition will put paid to any of your pretensions to good looks and a smooth countenance.'

'Thank you,' she replied acidly. 'I don't know that I've ever tried to claim that I was very good-looking.'

He leaned his elbows on the table and supported his chin on doubled fists. 'No? Well, you're no ugly duckling, true, although you don't come up to the level of Jaunty Julie. She's a stunner.'

'No one disputes that.'

'Still, you're not bad. Straight nose, even if it does turn up just that fraction. Your eyes—well, I can't see them if you don't look at me,' he complained.

'Why should I stare at you if I find something more worth while?' she demanded, giving him a childish, wide-eyed goggle, then turning her head to gaze around the restaurant.

'Hazel, I suppose you'd call them,' Brooke was saying. 'Like a stream running over greenish-brown stones. Your hair is pretty. Does it curl up at the ends by itself or do you twiddle it up at nights in curling pins?'

But Caran was scarcely listening to his left-handed compliments. On the far side of the room Julie sat alone at a table and as a waiter moved away from serving her, she glanced up and caught Caran's gaze.

'Julie's over the other side,' Caran told Brooke. 'I'd better ask her to join us.'

'No, don't do that——' Brooke began sharply, then he nodded. 'Yes, I'll ask the waiter.'

A few moments later Julie was sitting at a place between Caran and Brooke. 'What an unexpected meeting!' she exclaimed, glancing from one to the other.

From then on, Julie took charge of the conversation, talking almost exclusively to Brooke, with an occasional 'Don't you think so, Caran?' flung in the latter's direction.

For some unexplained reason Caran was irritated. She was accustomed to Julie's habit of annexing any male acquaintance whom Caran found amiable, and to inserting herself into a twosome and turning it not into a pleasant trio, but a new twosome that excluded Caran.

Now Caran recalled that hasty half-sentence of Brooke's— 'No, don't do that——' broken off abruptly. Did that mean that he had preferred Caran's company alone to sharing the lunch with a third person, even when that third party was Julie?

Caran smiled gently. At this moment such an idea seemed hardly likely, for he was leaning forward listening intently to Julie's vivacious chatter.

It was inevitable that when the lunch was over Brooke drove the two girls back to the villas. Julie wanted to follow up her new opportunity by accompanying Brooke to his villa, but Caran said brusquely, 'Brooke wants to get some sleep. He's been up for most of two nights at the irrigation place.' She was astounded to hear how harshly she had spoken.

Brooke passed a hand across his eyes. 'Yes, I could really do with a few hours' sleep. I have to be up there again early tomorrow morning.'

In the living room of the Villa Joyosa, Julie tossed her handbag on the table and flung herself into an armchair.

'That was rather a chopper coming down, wasn't it, darling?' She gave Caran an oblique, upward glance. 'What are you afraid of? That I might oust you with Brooke?'

'I've no fear of that,' replied Caran calmly. 'I was merely thinking of Brooke——'

'Obviously,' cut in Julie.

Caran sighed. 'Let me finish. There was a disastrous accident at the dam. He's been up there for several days and had no sleep or very little. He needs some rest before he goes to the site again.'

'In that case, I'm surprised he took you to lunch in the town.'

Caran laughed. 'He said he couldn't sleep until he'd eaten a proper meal.' She turned towards Julie. 'Besides, if he hadn't taken me to El Catalan, you wouldn't have had the chance of meeting him there, would you?'

Julie pouted. 'Not exactly the only chance, though, elusive though he may be.'

Caran took the cover off her typewriter. 'Will it disturb you if I type? I've some lists to do for Paul.'

'Don't bother about me. I shall probably go for a walk somewhere.'

'How did you get on about engaging the maids for the villas?' asked Caran.

Julie was on her way to the bedroom. 'Oh, that! I haven't got very far, but we've plenty of time to sort that out.'

Caran made no reply. She guessed that Julie had not bothered much about the addresses, but spent most of her time looking in the shops until it was time for lunch at El Catalan.

Caran was busy with her typing when Julie emerged again wearing a short fur jacket striped in black and cream.

'Like it?' she queried, pirouetting for Caran's benefit.

'M'm, very fetching. No one but you would dare to wear

horizontal stripes. Did you buy it here?'

Julie's brown eyes sparkled. 'Too pricey for me to buy. It's an advance Christmas present.'

'From Paul?'

'How clever of you to guess! There are times when I really think he's a pet.'

Caran laughed gently. 'The other day you were complaining about him,' she pointed out.

'The other day is now history. Time marches on and I'm always flexible enough to take what opportunities are offered to me.'

With that cryptic remark Julie sauntered out of the villa, leaving Caran to ponder over the astonishing ups and downs of Paul's relationship with Julie. Sometimes he appeared to be completely infatuated with Julie; at others he seemed bored or indifferent. Perhaps, thought Caran, the situation was quite simple; Paul and Julie understood each other in a sophisticated way that allowed for a certain freedom. In the past Julie had not hesitated to go out with other men while vowing that the particular man of the moment was really 'the one'.

When Julie had not returned by about nine o'clock, Caran was slightly alarmed. She had prepared dinner for the two of them and now decided that probably Julie was dining at one of the restaurants in the town. Caran ate her own meal and cleared away.

It was nearly eleven o'clock when Caran heard voices outside the villa and she hurried to the porch, switching on the inside lights.

Julie and Brooke stood there. 'Coming in for a drink?' asked Julie, but Brooke shook his head.

Julie turned towards Caran. 'Hope you weren't anxious about me, Caran. I know what you are for worrying. I've been in Brooke's villa and the time went by like a flash.'

'Sure you won't come in, Brooke?' Caran asked him.

'I've a spot of work to do. Just thought I'd see Julie back here.' To Caran he seemed to be smiling inanely at Julie. 'Those paths are rather dark.'

Julie giggled. 'Frightfully dark. Maybe it's intentional not to light them.'

When he had gone, Caran asked, 'Are you hungry, Julie? I could get you something.'

Julie stood pensively by the table. 'No, thanks. Brooke and I had a sort of picnic meal. He's so fascinating that I forgot all about dinner. He's quite a cook, too. Knocked up some concoction with tomatoes and onions and red peppers.'

'What time did you call on him then?' asked Caran.

'Time? Oh, I haven't the faintest idea. I walked along the shore for a while, but it was dreary, so I came back and I was passing Brooke's villa when he stepped out. Oh, I know what you're thinking. That I barged in, banging on his door and disturbing his precious nap. It was all quite by chance. Naturally he invited me in.'

Caran smiled. 'I suppose his place is untidy as ever.'

'Not really. Lots of books and papers about, of course, but apparently Benita, that dancing girl, goes in every afternoon to clean and tidy the villa.'

This was news to Caran. So Brooke succeeded in obtaining maid service quite independently of the management! Was this one more pointer to Brooke's involvement with the Spanish girl?

Julie moved restlessly about the room, then sat in an arm-chair, her fur jacket tossed on to another chair. 'I've been thinking about our position,' she began. 'I'd like to move into one of the other villas. The one called Esmeralda for prefer-ence. That's been redecorated, so there's no problem there.'

Caran was astounded. 'But you can't occupy a whole villa, especially Esmeralda. That's the largest of all.'

'Well, there are only two vacant at the moment, and the other one—which that Spanish family occupied—that has to be painted and so on.'

'But why do you want to move at all?' demanded Caran.

Julie shrugged. 'I'm cramped here. Sharing a bedroom is not ideal, you must admit.'

'But Esmeralda has four bedrooms. Paul hopes to let several villas for late February. The new ones will be fin-ished by then, we hope.'

'I'm not stopping him letting them now, am I?' Julie

spoke sharply. 'When he wants other people in them, I daresay some new arrangement can be found for me.'

'You'll probably have to return to this one. Obviously, I've been given the smallest of the lot, because I need to be on the spot without taking up too much accommodation. Have you told Paul that you want to change?'

'Oh, yes. He agrees entirely. He suggested Cristal, but I prefer Esmeralda.'

Caran made no further attempt to argue. Whatever Paul settled she would accept, but in the darkness of the bedroom when Julie slept, while Caran's eyelids would not close, she was aware that the Villa Esmeralda was next door to Zafiro, Brooke's villa. Julie was evidently all set for a determined attack on Brooke's susceptibilities. Caran would be interested to see how far Julie would succeed, for Brooke was a tougher proposition than the more usual type of man who was instantly drawn to a glamorous personality. The needling thought penetrated Caran's mind that she did not want Julie's victory to happen too soon. She told herself that a little opposition would do Julie good, even though she knew in her heart that conflict would merely spur Julie on to fresh efforts. Anyway, Caran was on the sidelines and not at all involved in that argument. For once, she wanted to see Julie defeated. Why? Because of Brooke? He had never treated her as anything but a useful companion and a verbal sparring partner. Why should she fret if he became one more captive to Julie's adroit technique with men? The question remained unanswered, for at last Caran had fallen asleep.

CHAPTER SIX

PAUL surprised the two girls next morning by saying that he had arranged to take them to lunch with Don Ramiro in Almeria the following day.

'I thought I'd better give you a day's notice and not spring it on you both,' he said. 'Dress yourselves up to the eyebrows, for this is a special occasion.'

'I'm told he has a very fine house, a small palace, in fact,' observed Caran.

'Yes, very stylish,' agreed Paul.

'I suppose we must go tomorrow?' queried Julie. 'Why not one day next week?'

Paul looked shocked. 'My dearest Julie, this is almost a royal command! You don't quibble about dates when Don Ramiro invites you to his mansion.'

'Oh, I see. A business lunch and you're taking us along to stop it all getting too boring. All right, I'll dig out something not too dowdy, although I'd have preferred an opportunity to buy something special—if that's possible in this part of Spain.'

Julie was evidently irritated by Paul's suggestion, and Caran wondered if the other girl had been intending to try to consolidate her newly-won friendship with Brooke in the scant time he might spare from his work.

When the three set out next morning for Almeria, Julie looked enchanting in a glowing violet wool dress, which made a dashing contrast to her red-gold hair. The black and cream fur jacket and a small cream fur hat, with black bag and gloves, completed her outfit. Beside her, Caran in a gentian blue dress topped by a plain cream coat knew her appearance to be humdrum. She felt like the humble companion to an exotic film or television star.

Paul, however, eyed his two associates with approval and as he drove to Almeria chatted about a dozen topics. Julie sat in the back seat, explaining that she did not want to crease her skirt unduly. Caran, left to sit next to Paul, gathered that Julie's skirt was not of such prime importance as the fact that she wanted to keep a little distance between herself and Paul.

The house of the Mendosa family was situated in a main street leading out of the town and some short distance from the sea and harbour. Paul drove through a white stone gateway with handsome black iron gates into a courtyard with Moorish arches, then through a central arch into a patio where small fountains played. Even though this was December, roses and geraniums flourished in tubs or small raised beds. Along the balconies of each of the two storeys trailed vines and creepers, bougainvillea and sprays of creamy flowers.

Don Ramiro came out to greet his guests. He wore an immaculate light grey suit with a paler grey shirt; his dark hair was smoothed so that it resembled a shining cap. Caran was unexpectedly reminded of Brooke's usual contrasting untidiness.

Don Ramiro now smiled graciously as he kissed Caran's hand, greeted Paul, who introduced Julie. Then he led the way into his imposing, ancient house.

The initial effect was almost overpowering, thought Caran. The high vaulted roof of the hall was surprising, towering up to a dark-beamed ceiling hung with bronze and crystal lanterns that shed a soft, mellow light on to stone walls. A huge table of almost black wood, some ornately carved high-back chairs, a painted shield above the fireplace—these details Caran noticed as Don Ramiro ushered his guests into another adjoining room. This was evidently the family dining-room with panelled walls richly carved and tall french windows opening on to yet another patio.

A long table was laid with more than half a dozen places and Caran wondered who the other guests would be. She was almost immediately answered by the entrance of a small, but imperious-looking woman in black silk, whom Don Ramiro introduced as his mother, Señora Juanita Eulalia Joaquina de Colomer y del Coso y Mendosa. Caran, lost among this string of names, smiled and waited for the older woman to extend a dainty hand so frail that Caran merely touched it with the utmost gentleness.

In a few moments three more women entered the room, obviously Spanish and of different ages. Don Ramiro introduced them as his cousins Mirella, Fernanda and Iñez. They, too, had long strings of names for formal occasions, no doubt. Mirella was the youngest and prettiest of the trio, with a serenely beautiful face, a pale skin, luminous dark eyes and masses of long black hair. Caran guessed she might be about nineteen or twenty. The other two were in their thirties, probably, and members of Don Ramiro's household.

His mother now sat at the head of the oblong table and the long luncheon began. 'Luncheon' was a word that Caran usually disdained to use for a midday meal, however grand, but today's event really deserved the name. So many delicious little dishes, fish cooked in wine, small pieces of meat wrapped in thin pastry, red and green peppers served with a tangy sauce, to the final stages of frosted grapes and other fruit and a dozen varieties of cheese.

Señora Mendosa spoke little English, but was voluble in her own language and seemed gratified that Caran could follow her with reasonable ease, although Caran found her pronunciation deserting her at crucial moments. At the same time, Don Ramiro was aware of Julie's lack of Spanish and Paul's incomplete grasp of the language, and the result was a hotch-potch of Anglo-Spanish back and forth across the table and the two older cousins joining in with an occasional *'Es verdad?'*—if they doubted the truth of what was said.

After lunch, Señora Mendosa and the three cousins retired, but Don Ramiro conducted his three guests to part of the patio where they could sit among orange and lemon trees and enjoy their coffee and liqueurs.

To Caran's surprise, Paul spoke very little of his business projects. She had imagined that perhaps he required Don Ramiro's help, although in what way she had no idea. All the same, it was Don Ramiro who had both influence and wealth and could probably make or break any intending speculator on the whole coast from Almeria to Alicante.

'Perhaps you would like to stroll around our gardens?'

Don Ramiro suggested after some time, and Caran was a little astonished to find herself tucking her hand into his proffered elbow like some courtly lady at Versailles.

At some point or other in this magnificent garden of flowering bushes, spiky cacti and oleanders, Paul and Julie seemed to have fallen behind and now Caran and Don Ramiro were alone. This was the opportunity she had been waiting for.

'I must thank you very much indeed for finding a house for the family who had to take refuge in one of our villas,' she said.

'The family?' After a moment's thought, his frown cleared. 'Ah, yes, I remember. They occupied one of your villas.'

'Gabriela and her family have gone.' She glanced up at him. 'I'm sure you must have spoken for them and I'm glad. But I can't find out their new address. Do you know?'

He paused in their sedate pacing. 'Perhaps it is better not to know,' he told her, his dark eyes dancing with amusement. 'If you credit me with a good action, then I am afraid you might be disappointed if you know too much of the truth.'

'Well, as long as they are comfortably settled,' said Caran, as they resumed their strolling.

Don Ramiro plied her with questions about her work at the villas. She answered some quite candidly, but when he touched on the subject of development, she gave cautious replies. For all she knew, Paul did not want his secrets disclosed.

'Personally, I think it a pity to spoil such a lovely place as Albarosa with the usual tourist paraphernalia of towering hotels and beach umbrellas and swimming pools,' she said.

'Spain must look forward as well as backward to its history,' he murmured as though his thoughts were on something else. Then he asked, 'Why don't you like our excellent seaside resorts?'

'I didn't say that. I'm all in favour of many such places being developed. I just don't want them all to look alike. But of course, you have much influence in Albarosa, I understand. You wouldn't allow anything unsightly to be built there.'

'I assure you, Señorita Caran, that nothing shall ever be built on my land that you might consider unsightly, nor shall I allow others to do so. There! You have extracted from me a promise which I would not like to break.'

They were now close to the stables and an occasional whinny or thump of hoof broke the afternoon silence.

Suddenly Don Ramiro took both of Caran's hands in his own.

'I have given you much thought since I saw you last,' he said, his voice vibrant and low. 'We have not met often enough and I would like to know you better. You English girls have so much more freedom than ours, even though we do not keep them chained up in convents or surround them with so many restrictions as formerly. But you have more understanding of men because you are more free.'

Caran felt herself colouring. 'Our freedom is something that nowadays we take for granted, but I don't know if it gives us more understanding of men.'

'Oh, but yes.' His dark eyes drew her like a magnet, yet there was something in their depths that alarmed her. 'There is a quality you have that I have not met before. Since the night I first saw you at the airport I have tried to analyse it, but I have failed.'

She tugged gently at her hands within his clasp, but he held them the more firmly. 'Don Ramiro——' she began softly.

Suddenly he released her hands as though they were burning him. 'Forgive me, Señorita Caran, I am behaving very impolitely. It is not usual for me to treat my guests so. Come, I will show you the place in our garden where you can catch a glimpse of the Sierra Nevada.'

Caran hardly knew what to make of this abrupt *volte-face*, but recovered her poise. She and Don Ramiro had walked only a couple of steps to the corner of the stable block when they came face to face with Paul and Julie accompanied by Mirella, the youngest cousin.

'Oh, we thought we'd lost you!' Paul said to Caran.

'It is easy to lose oneself in our rambling garden,' remarked Don Ramiro, and Caran thought she detected a slight double meaning in his words.

The lovely Mirella smiled serenely at Caran, who now wondered if Don Ramiro had broken off his conversation a few moments ago because he had caught a whisper of other voices close by.

Today the atmosphere was clear and the snow-capped sierras appeared deceptively near.

'In summer,' observed Mirella, 'we become very hot, so we come to this part of the garden to look at the snow on Nevada.'

On the way home, Julie decided to sit with Paul, a strategic position from which she could talk to the driver and half turn round to include Caran. Julie was in a teasing mood.

'Spain has already done wonders for you, darling,' she remarked. 'You've acquired poise and sophistication in a way I wouldn't have thought possible.'

'Thank you,' murmured Caran. 'I can't do better than try to follow your example.'

Julie's trilling laugh held an undercurrent of derision. 'Even I could never have hit it off so well with the most handsome Spanish Don I've ever seen. It was awesome to watch you.'

'I didn't make any secret about Don Ramiro. In fact, I told you when you first came that I had a Spanish Don up my sleeve. Remember?' For once Caran was enjoying Julie's slight discomfiture.

'Caran knows how to get on well with all sorts of important people,' interposed Paul. 'I was very glad indeed to see Don Ramiro taking such an interest in you. Why, you had him practically eating out of your hand.'

'Out in the garden he was taking immense interest in your hands,' continued Julie. 'You were almost in his arms. Did he kiss you before we arrived?'

Caran laughed. 'You two seem to sum up the situation to your own satisfaction. Why should I disclose anything you might have missed?'

'There, Paul!' Julie said. 'See what I mean? Once upon a

time Caran would have blushed, and mumbled denials all along the line. Now she neatly parries questions she doesn't want to answer.'

Caran remained silent and the conversation drifted to other topics, but later Julie shook a warning finger at Caran. 'That girl Mirella—I thought she had rather a beady look whenever Don Ramiro was around. Do you think she could possibly be the intended bride that the family has selected for him?'

'I've never met her until today, so how could I know?' asked Caran.

'All the same, pet, have your fun, but I'd advise you not to become too involved with the Spanish *caballero*.'

'Oh, I don't know about that. If you were warned off someone, that would make you only the keener to capture him.'

Julie gave a throaty chuckle. 'Possibly, but then I'm much tougher than you. Really, I wouldn't like you to get hurt.'

'Oh, Caran can take good care of herself,' put in Paul. 'She knows how to play her cards.'

In the back of the car Caran really wondered what hand of cards she had played after lunch. What particular words or action of hers had incited Don Ramiro to that brief, romantic interlude?

Caran knew that in another moment, if he had not sensed the interruption, he would have drawn her into his arms. But why? She could only imagine that perhaps a trifle more wine at lunch had excited his senses, for he was surely not the type of man to hug and kiss any girl near at hand.

When she and Julie were preparing for bed, Julie thumped her pillows and said casually, 'I've a completely clear conscience now.'

'In what respect?' queried Caran, idly brushing her hair.

'In respect of you, darling. Now that I know you have Don Ramiro on a string, I feel free in other directions.'

'Meaning Paul? Or Brooke?'

Julie's mouth curled in a delicious smile, the lovely smile that was so engaging in the advertisements she had posed for. 'Does it matter which? I've told you that Paul doesn't interest me except as a convenient escort when one is necessary.'

'I see. Point taken,' murmured Caran. It was on the tip of her tongue to say with the utmost flippancy, 'Go ahead ! See if you can twist Brooke around your little finger !' But that would have been a definite challenge to Julie, who could easily conquer without such incitement.

'Extraordinary,' continued Julie, 'how everyone used to think Brooke a recluse, a stuffed owl engrossed with his work and nothing else. At least, that's what Paul told me. Brooke isn't like that at all, is he?'

'There are times when he doesn't like to be disturbed,' returned Caran cautiously. 'When he's here in the villa, he has a lot of work to do, records to keep, and translation of instructions for the men.' She was not going to fall into the trap of admitting that when he chose to exert himself she found him a most congenial companion. Yet she had not forgotten that first encounter when she had mistaken his villa for her own. He had behaved like a hermit crab then.

The next morning Julie packed a good many of her clothes in the numerous suitcases she had brought with her and prepared to move into the Villa Esmeralda.

'How did you manage to bring so much with you on the plane?' asked Caran. 'Excess baggage?'

'Excess indeed, and what I had to pay for it !' groaned Julie.

Caran accompanied her to Esmeralda, helped her to settle in and explained the heating.

'Make the most of it, Julie. When the first visitors come, you'll have to live in a bathing hut on the beach.'

'We'll see,' replied Julie smugly.

Late in the afternoon Paul came to see Caran. 'What's all this about Julie moving into Esmeralda?'

'But you knew about it, Paul. She told you.'

He shook his head. 'It's the first I've heard of it. She says it was your idea because you felt cramped and wanted this villa to yourself.'

'Rubbish !' said Caran tersely. 'Julie's the one who felt cramped.' She did not add that Julie wanted to be next door to Brooke. Paul would have to find that out for himself.

'Oh, well, she can stay there for the time being, I suppose. But now that it's redecorated and all shipshape, I wanted to keep that one as a special showpiece.'

'Julie's untidy, but not messy or destructive,' Caran pointed out in the other girl's defence, 'and of course she understands it's only a temporary move.'

Paul shrugged acceptance of the situation and spoke of other matters. 'We must have maids,' he said testily. 'Surely there must be *some* girl in the town who'd be glad to do a little light housework in return for good wages.'

'I'll see what I can do,' promised Caran, remembering Señora Molina with whom she had stayed that first night in Albarosa.

'Another thing—I more or less invited Don Ramiro to a Christmas Eve dinner here. Do you think you could manage a typical Christmas spread?'

'An English Christmas? Turkey and plum pudding and all that? It's terribly short notice, with Christmas only three days away.' Caran was annoyed that Paul had not mentioned this idea sooner.

'I'll see that you have all the ingredients and trimmings,' Paul coaxed her. 'It'll be an eye-opener for the Don to see our kind of feast.'

'It'll be an eye-opener all right,' agreed Caran grimly, 'especially if the turkey is tough and the pudding indigestible.'

'Let me have a list of what you want and I'll have everything delivered,' Paul told her, patting her on the back with friendly encouragement.

'I think I'd better do the shopping myself tomorrow morning,' she suggested. 'Then I shall know what substitutes will do if the shops haven't got exactly what I want. I might also tackle someone I know about the possibility of maids.'

Caran wanted to do some shopping alone the next day, for she had presents to buy for Gabriela and the children, although she did not yet know where they were living. Perhaps at Christmas Benita would be more forthcoming and helpful.

She had to guess at the sizes of dresses for the various children, but the shopkeepers were helpful and there was no difficulty at all in buying a couple of dresses that she was sure would fit Gabriela.

The shops were gay with Christmas decorations, coloured candles with streamers. Some windows held a traditional crib, but more elaborate than Caran had usually seen, for these were surrounded by the features of a village, a mill, a well and a silver-paper river spanned by matchstick bridges. Many little Christmas trees appeared and in almost every food shop there were displays of marzipan serpents eating their own tails.

Caran made some purchases in the shop where Benita worked and as she discussed the quality of sultanas and raisins, she handed over the parcels to Benita.

'These are some small Christmas gifts for your sister and her children. If I knew where they lived——'

'Oh, *no*,' said Benita hastily, but then smiled. 'Forgive me, that is ungrateful. Gabriela will be very pleased.'

'There are dolls for the youngest girls and a paintbox for the older one and several model cars for the boys. I didn't know what else to get.' Caran had remembered the pathetic little rag doll that one of the children had left behind in the Villa Cristal.

'Señorita Caran, you are very kind. Like Señor Brooke. He also is kind to us.'

'Then why don't you trust me and give me Gabriela's address?'

Benita shook her head. 'Not yet. Perhaps later.'

Caran had to be content with that half-promise. She paid for her purchases and went to the house of Señora Molina.

The older woman pursed her lips and shook her head emphatically when Caran explained that the villas needed maids for the spring and summer.

'Not possible,' she told Caran. 'I do not know of girls who might come.'

'Is it because the villas have a bad reputation?' Caran asked bluntly. It was better to know exactly what she was up against.

Señora Molina smiled. 'The villas are away from the town, you understand. Many tourists come, all nationalities, and the mothers do not like their daughters to be so far away in a lonely place.'

'If it were a hotel down there, would the girls come?'

'Perhaps. Yes, it is more likely.'

After a pause Caran said, 'This year I shall be supervising the maids in the villas and I shall make sure that they do not work more than the five or six hours a day for which they are engaged.'

Señora Molina sighed. 'If I can help you, I will do so. Perhaps it is good that you will look after the girls, although you are very young yourself.'

Caran smiled. 'Old enough to know that the maids must have good conditions.' That was not quite what she meant, but she knew that the older woman would comprehend, even in Caran's rather faulty Spanish, that Caran would do everything she could to protect the girls from unwelcome attentions.

On the way back she reflected that Paul had really bedevilled the situation by frightening Benita, who in turn had warned off everyone else.

Or was Brooke just as bad? The sudden thought halted Caran in mid-stride. He was on excellent terms with Benita, who kept his villa clean, if not tidy; he gave her flamenco dresses. What else? Yet Benita liked and trusted Brooke, whereas apparently she detested Paul.

Was there another reason why Benita wanted to keep other girls away from the villas by alarming them? If she wanted to enjoy Brooke's friendship to the full she might not want to risk sharing it with other girls from her own town.

Caran gave it up. She could only hope for the best and in any case, the problem could be shelved until after Christmas.

On the morning of Christmas Eve Julie announced that she had invited Brooke to dinner that evening.

'I simply couldn't let the poor lamb eat an omelette or dine in the town when we're stuffing ourselves.'

'I was going to invite the "poor lamb" anyway,' replied Caran, 'if he wanted to come and had nothing better to do.'

But Paul was intensely annoyed, it seemed. 'I've specially asked Don Ramiro to come over to sample our English Christmas, and now you two upset what should have been a pleasant foursome.'

'I'm sorry, Paul,' Caran apologised, 'but if you and Don Ramiro want to talk business matters, I'm sure Julie and I will oblige and take Brooke out of earshot.'

Julie laughed gaily. 'If you're not careful, Paul, you'll find yourself alone smoking a cigar and downing wine, while Caran has annexed Don Ramiro in some quiet corner and Brooke and I have gone down to the shore to listen to the sad sea waves.'

Caran joined in the laughter, but secretly she hoped that the pairings would not turn out like that. She had no desire for a cosy tête-à-tête with Don Ramiro; she liked still less the idea of Julie and Brooke walking hand in hand, or even closer, by the shore. She dismissed the silly notion. Anyone would think she was becoming jealous about Brooke!

The Christmas Eve dinner turned out to be a happy occasion. Caran took immense trouble with every item of the meal, the turkey which Paul had miraculously procured from somewhere.

There should really be cranberry sauce, she explained to Don Ramiro, but she had been forced to make do with some bottled redcurrants. The traditional pudding was a revelation to him, especially when brandy was lavishly poured over it and set alight.

'You have excellent traditions in your country,' he said politely. 'I have never eaten such a splendid dinner.'

'The best Christmas dinner I've had this year,' Brooke commented with a glance at Caran.

Before Caran could even say thank you for the compliments, Julie said, 'Well, it's marvellous to hear your praises. Caran and I worked really hard, didn't we, pet?'

Since Julie had not so much as peeled a vegetable and her assistance had been limited to adding the finishing touches to the table, Caran was lost for a reply, but decided it didn't matter.

Over the rim of his wineglass Paul slanted Caran a smiling glance that said plainly, 'Don't mind if Julie wants to take half the credit. I know the truth.'

He, too, had worked hard to obtain various Christmas trimmings, including a box of crackers from some unknown source.

As they were now passed round with the port, they caused a few minutes of hilarious amusement.

Brooke, wearing a bright pink crown that fitted badly on his thick hair, was unravelling his motto. 'I'll bet it warns me about crossing water in case I meet a blonde gipsy. There! What did I tell you? Listen to this.

' "Water is your enemy, wine your friend,
If she loves another, what matter the end?" '

Caran shivered slightly at the reference to water being Brooke's enemy, but Don Ramiro was reading his little slip of paper.

' "If you would find a heart that's true
Then seek the girl who longs for you." '

'A fine bit of doggerel, that!' commented Paul.

Don Ramiro glanced at Caran with an intensity that forced her to turn her head away.

'Come on, Caran!' urged Brooke. 'Let's hear yours.'

' "Light and bright and gay as day
Whirl your worries all away," '

she read aloud. 'Another bit of awful doggerel.'

Paul and Julie received equally inane couplets.

'How on earth did you manage to get these English crackers here in Spain?' Julie asked Paul, pushing aside the red paper hat which she decided would not accord with her hair.

'Simple!' He gave her a beaming smile. 'I asked my aunt to send them.'

Don Ramiro had arranged to stay the night at the house of his friend Señora Molina, so that he would not have to drive all the way back to Almeria. Before he left he thanked Caran for all the trouble she had taken.

'You must come to us for New Year,' he invited, then added belatedly, 'All of you, of course.'

'Sorry about that, Don Ramiro,' said Brooke quietly, 'but I have a prior engagement for New Year's Eve. So has Caran.'

'I? What engagement is that?' she asked.

'We must eat our twelve grapes at midnight.'

Don Ramiro smiled. 'Of course, but Caran could eat her grapes in my house just as easily as in yours.'

Brooke shook his head. 'I asked first, but Caran will do as she wishes.'

'We shall have to let you know about the arrangements, Don Ramiro,' broke in Caran, trying to make peace between the two men over what seemed an entirely insignificant matter.

When Don Ramiro had driven away in his car, Julie was curious to know what was so important about grape-eating on New Year's Eve.

'It's an old Spanish custom,' answered Paul. 'You eat a grape for each of the coming twelve months. Brings you luck, I suppose.'

'It has more meaning than that,' said Brooke. 'Still, it's unimportant. I shan't complain wherever you choose to eat your grapes, Caran.'

Brooke's tone seemed suddenly cold, and Caran wondered why he had made such an issue of so small a point.

'I'll let you know this important place in due course,' she said in as cool a tone as his.

'I know where I shall eat mine,' declared Julie. 'Wherever Brooke happens to be.'

The look he gave her seemed to Caran to be compounded of fatuous admiration and a certain objective appraisal of Julie's willingness to accede to a demand that he had not so far asked of her.

It was natural that he should accompany Julie to her villa, since it was on the way to his own, but Caran's imagination accompanied them on that short journey through the dark garden paths and she was angry with herself for harbouring such foolish thoughts. She went out to the kitchen to tackle the washing up.

'Oh, leave it until the morning,' called Paul. 'Come and sit with me for a few minutes.'

Caran obeyed, glad to postpone a mundane task until she felt less tired.

Paul knocked the ash off his cigar. 'What do you think about Julie?' he asked after a moment or two.

'What about her?'

'I mean—do you think she's really falling for Brooke?'

'You can't ever tell with Julie,' replied Caran. 'She often manages to make it look as though she's desperately in love with someone, but it soon wears off if someone new appears. Oh, Paul, I don't want that to sound accusing or unkind,' she added hastily.

He smiled. 'Oh, I realise what I'm up against. The fact is I've been thinking that she and I would make a rattling good partnership in every way, business, marriage—all round.'

Caran noticed immediately that he had placed business first before marriage and had not even mentioned love.

'She has marvellous looks,' continued Paul, 'and behind that apparent flippancy she has intelligence and a smart brain. If matters here go as I'm planning, there should be plenty of scope for all of us. I'm a bit worried, though, about Eldridge. He used to seem such a crusty sort of bachelor when I was here last year. Now he's juggling about with all the girls. I've an idea that he has Benita on a string, a willing little slave and all that.'

'I don't know about that,' observed Caran. 'Benita goes into the villa to clean for him and dust. I daresay she often brings home some food for him, to save his time in shopping. But about Julie—if I were you, Paul, I'd play it cool. She responds to a touch of indifference now and again.'

He smiled suddenly at her. 'The way you play it so cool with Don Ramiro. I have to hand it to you, Caran. Your technique is wonderful. I never imagined that a haughty Mendosa would fall so completely for an English girl like you.'

Caran laughed. 'Your imagination is working overtime. I don't believe the haughty Mendosa has done anything of the sort.'

'Oh, but he has,' said Paul emphatically. 'Keep it up, Caran dear. Don't spoil it for all our sakes. I reckon that if you wanted it you could easily be Señora Caran Mendosa. Think of it! All those estates he owns!'

'A castle in Spain?' she queried.

'A small palace in Almeria, a villa here in Albarosa and heaven knows what else.'

'An old ruined castle between here and Matana,' she told him. 'At least Brooke said it was once a stronghold of the Mendosas.'

Paul rose and stretched himself. 'Well, I must go. See you tomorrow. Oh, yes, it's already Christmas Day. Happy Christmas, Caran.' He bent towards her and kissed her lips. At the door on his way out, he turned as she accompanied him. 'It might be a good thing if you accepted Don Ramiro's invitation for New Year's Eve.'

'For the grapes?'

'For everything,' he answered. 'Good night.'

Caran shut the outer door and leaned against it. The idea of Paul's inciting her to try to marry Don Ramiro was ludicrous in the extreme. What did Paul hope to gain from such a marriage of convenience? A business concession, perhaps, but no doubt that could be obtained by astute bargaining without involving Caran in a matchmaking endeavour.

So in Paul's calculations she was to be paired off with Don Ramiro, while he captured Julie. Only Brooke was left out of their tidy quartet, but would he submit to that? Supposing it was Julie who appropriated Brooke and he was willing to be thus shackled?

Caran deliberately swung her thoughts away from this prospect, for she found herself hoping that it would never happen.

CHAPTER SEVEN

On Christmas morning Caran walked up to the town. The streets were quiet, the bars closed and silent. Albarosa seemed to be wrapped in a sombre mist. The inhabitants were no doubt resting after last night's feast, then midnight Mass, followed by the clangour and booming of rattles and *zambombas*. She had seen and heard these archaic instruments when Brooke had taken her to the fiesta in the mountains. Shaped like earthenware flower-pots, they were open at one end while the other was covered with a piece of parchment with a hole into which a reed was inserted. By rubbing a wetted finger up and down the reed, an astonishingly loud *rom, rom, rom* sound was produced. Last night long after she was in bed she could hear the distant thumping of the *zambombas*.

Now she passed the doctor's house where his balconies, rising in tiers for three storeys, were always a mass of flowers; lilies and geraniums, trails of jasmine and creepers wreathed the ironwork. She knew the plan of the town fairly well by now and in daylight at least could walk anywhere without losing herself.

She went down a narrow alley on the far side of the town where it sloped inland away from the sea. From a wide double doorway emerged a child clutching a doll. Caran's attention was first caught by the doll, then she looked intently at the child. Surely one of Gabriela's small daughters? The little girl glanced up, smiled shyly in half recognition, then ran through the doorway.

Caran hesitated for a moment or two, then followed. A donkey tethered in one corner stared with patient, incurious eyes. A smaller door stood ajar and Caran found herself in a narrow yard. A wooden shack occupied most of the space. Was this hovel the place that Don Ramiro had found for the family?

Her unspoken question was answered by Gabriela herself,

who came out of the shack with a bucket of dirty water. When she saw Caran she jerked back with shocked surprise and the water slopped over the edge of the pail.

'What do you want here?' Gabriela whispered, her dark eyes wide with mingled terror and shame.

Caran smiled. 'Don't be angry, Gabriela. I saw one of your little daughters holding the doll—I think it was one I sent, so I came to see where you live.'

Gabriela bowed her head as she set down the bucket. 'We have done what you asked, but it is only for a time. Then we shall have something better.'

'Don Ramiro has promised he will find you a house?'

Gabriela's head came up sharply. 'Don Ramiro? Oh, no. The English Señor Brooke. He is good to us.'

'Good!' Caran's voice was scornful. Why couldn't he have let them stay a little longer in the Villa Cristal instead of bringing them to this outhouse behind a stable? Aloud she said gently, 'Are you comfortable inside there?' She knew it was a ludicrous question, but she must persuade Gabriela to show her the interior.

Gabriela's face responded with a slightly less tense expression. 'It was kind of you to send the gifts for us, the clothes and the toys. Felipe, too, is most grateful.'

'Let me come in and see the children, Gabriela,' Caran pleaded.

The other woman yielded after a moment's inner struggle against her pride. 'You understand it is only for a week or two? After that——' her voice trailed away.

'If Señor Eldridge—Señor Brooke—has promised, then you can rely on him,' Caran assured her. Although she was angry with Brooke for keeping her in the dark about this move, she knew that any promises by Don Ramiro or Paul would probably have been conveniently unfulfilled once the Ribera family were out of the villa.

When she saw the inside of this hut she was amazed at the homelike atmosphere Gabriela had achieved. Felipe sat at a wooden table scrubbed to whiteness and was employed in painting little animals and figures fashioned out of some putty-like substance. When he saw Caran he jumped to his feet, offered her his chair, the only one at present in the hut.

'For the children?' she asked, pointing to the little toy figures of elephant and donkey and an endearing, long-necked giraffe.

He nodded and explained that he obtained scraps of clay from a builder friend and let the toys dry in the sun.

One end of the hut was partitioned off with a curtain which Gabriela now lifted to show Caran the part where the children slept, a makeshift bed consisting of two chairs and a hollow wooden box. Inside the base of the box was a small bundle of coverings, so apparently one child slept there, the rest on the floor.

The wooden walls were scrupulously clean and at the side of the tiny window hung a little statuette of the Virgin Mary.

'But you and Felipe?' asked Caran delicately. 'You have no place to sleep?'

Gabriela smiled. 'Oh, yes. At night we go into the stable. The man who owns the donkey does not mind.'

Sharing a stable with a donkey, reflected Caran sadly. Yet it occurred to her that this was Christmas Day and possibly it was appropriate to discover that there were still people who would accept with humility a small share of such a lodging when there was no room elsewhere. At the same time she was now determined to make every effort to house this family in better accommodation, even if she paid the rent herself.

'I have not seen you at the restaurant El Catalan,' she said to Felipe.

'I was ill for some days,' he answered slowly, 'and the proprietor did not want me back again when I recovered. It was only a bad cold.'

No wonder, thought Caran, sleeping in a draughty stable.

'But now I shall not have colds, for Señor Brooke has given me warm clothes,' he continued happily.

So Benita had passed on Brooke's cast-offs. That was something.

'Then you're not working now?' she queried gently.

'Oh, yes. In the shop where Benita is. I take in the stores and put them on the shelves and then I deliver some of the orders.'

Caran was worried. She had seen men pushing handcarts in the streets, delivering goods from one place to another. True, the town was hilly with narrow alleys unsuitable for vans or cars, but pushing a handcart over rough cobbles or unpaved streets was no light task. Nor, as far as Felipe's frail strength was concerned, was it child's play to drag boxes and cartons and sometimes barrels into the shop.

She drank the thimbleful of wine that Gabriela offered, knowing that a refusal would be hurtful, said goodbye to the five children, all neatly dressed, three of them in dresses Caran had bought. Now that she knew the address, she promised to come again soon.

'You will not tell anyone where we live?' queried Gabriela, haunting fear in her eyes.

'No, of course not. I'll keep it secret,' Caran assured her. 'Señor Brooke and I will do our best to find you a really pleasant place to live.'

When she returned to Joyosa, Julie came sauntering up the path.

'Where have you been all this time? I called ages ago, but I thought you weren't up yet after last night's orgy.'

'I went for a stroll in the town,' answered Caran.

'Any chance of lunch? Paul says that most restaurants and cafés are closed today.'

'I'll open a couple of tins of something,' agreed Caran. 'A little fasting might do both our waistlines a power of good.'

In Caran's living room Julie pottered about restlessly, while Caran was busy in the kitchen preparing a simple meal.

'What's the matter with you, Julie?' Caran called out. 'Why don't you relax?'

Julie came to the kitchen door. 'Relax? Impossible for me this morning. Here, take a look at this.' She fingered a necklace of oval amber-coloured beads, each one linked by delicate silver filigree.

Caran inspected the necklace lying against Julie's white

throat. 'Very handsome. Christmas present?'

Julie nodded. 'From Brooke.'

Caran dropped a spoon with a clatter on to the sink top.

'What did he give you?' Julie asked. 'Not a replica of this, I hope.'

Caran had mastered herself after that momentary surprise. 'Not a replica of anything,' she answered with a smile.

'Oh!' Julie's brown eyes widened. 'Then that's why—well, you see, darling, why I simply can't relax at this moment. If Brooke had also given you a—well, a token, shall we say?—then I'd have known that he treats all the girls alike. But not to give you anything—that was mean. I'm not sure now whether he really wants me to take him seriously.'

'You once advised me never to take any man seriously until he's actually proposed marriage. Has Brooke?'

Julie simpered. 'Not yet. But I know he will. That's why I really wanted to make sure. You know, Caran, I wouldn't like you to be hurt over this affair.'

'Is it an affair, Julie?'

'Oh, no, I didn't mean exactly that,' Julie answered quickly. 'I meant——'

'There's no need to spare my feelings,' interrupted Caran, stirring onions, tomatoes and ham in a frying pan. 'I'm not in love with Brooke, if that's what you mean.'

Julie gave an enormously exaggerated sigh of apparent relief.

'Then that's a load off my mind,' she said.

As she dished up the lunch Caran asked quietly, 'When will you tell Paul?'

'Paul? Oh, he'll know soon enough,' replied Julie airily. 'By the way, did Paul give you a Christmas present?'

'Yes. A handsome bottle of perfume called "Ilusion".'

Julie's laughter tinkled. 'So safe! Dear Paul.'

Caran set the plates on the table. 'Why "Dear Paul"? You've no consideration for him. As far as you're concerned, he can sink or swim.'

'Oh, Caran, don't let's quarrel! Not about men! Nor on Christmas Day.'

'I'm sorry,' mumbled Caran. 'I feel sympathetic about

him, that's all.'

'No need. Paul's had a few rebuffs before now. He soon recovers.'

Caren thought that was probably true. In some ways, he and Julie were two of a kind, attracted like magnets to this girl or that man, then speedily breaking free when a more powerful attraction came along.

'There is one thing, though,' murmured Julie after a few minutes. 'Brooke will have to change his job. I shan't expect him to go about paddling in mud or concrete or whatever it is.'

'He'll be only too delighted to secure himself a cosy office job with half a dozen desk telephones. He'll wear well-cut suits and drive a shiny black car.'

Julie set down her fork and stared at Caran. 'You really are nettled about this, aren't you?'

Caran was angry with herself for letting her tongue run on like that. 'Not really, but I don't think women should try to interfere with men's chosen professions. If you fall in love, you fall in love with the whole man, job and all, not a reformed and tidy version of what you think he ought to be.'

'Dear, dear, what a lecture! Well, I've left you a perfectly free choice between two men whose jobs you wouldn't want to change. Paul will become a most successful property tycoon. As for Don Ramiro, no girl in her senses would want to alter one little bit of his way of life.'

Caran smiled. 'I'm not thinking of either of them in terms of husband-material. Nor of Brooke, for that matter,' she added hastily, seeing that she had left her defences wide open again to Julie's thrusts.

When the two girls had finished lunch Caran cleared away but was surprised when Julie offered to dry the dishes. Was there some further discussion or information that Julie wanted to talk about?

'Odd sort of Christmas Day, isn't it?' she remarked. 'Most of the gaiety happens at New Year, so I'm told.'

'Same as in Scotland.' Caran thought this some prelude to further conversation, but apparently Julie either changed her mind or had nothing further to add.

'I'll go along to Brooke's villa,' suggested Julie. 'We can always play snakes and ladders if we've nothing else better to do.'

The implication was not lost on Caran, and Julie's tone left no doubt that Caran was excluded from this afternoon visit.

Caran went into her bedroom and sat in front of the dressing-table mirror to appraise herself. Am I really jealous of Julie? Or is it merely pique because Brooke is so adept at dividing his favours? Selfishly, she wished with all her heart that Julie had not come to Albarosa, or if she had, then only for a holiday terminating in a departure date. Julie was now here indefinitely, an open-ended arrangement which left her free of commitment or responsibility. So far she was not on the pay-roll, but no doubt that would come. Paul would see to that and probably offer Julie generous salary terms as an inducement to stay.

Still, if Julie stayed on to please herself, she could not continue always to occupy the villa next to Brooke's. Esmeralda would be needed for tourists, along with Turquesa where Paul was staying, so new arrangements would be necessary.

Caran faced her reflected hazel eyes in the mirror. If Brooke was stupid enough to become ensnared by Julie's charms, surely he had only himself to blame. Caran asked herself why she should bother her head about yet another of Julie's conquests, but the answer came sharply. This was different. This was Brooke Eldridge and Caran believed that she knew Julie's tactics better than he did. Caran was forced to admit to herself that this time she cared about what injury Julie inflicted on a man's affections.

A further question pierced her mind. Why should she care? Brooke was surely capable of looking after himself without Caran's protection, but the question was not one to which she could offer a convincing answer.

She did not see Brooke again until New Year's Eve and then only for a minute or two as he hurried from the car park to his villa. 'See you tonight?' he queried. 'The grapes, remember?'

'Possibly,' she answered non-committally. She remembered Don Ramiro's invitation for tonight, but he had done nothing to renew it and it was too far to take the journey to Almeria merely to eat a few grapes.

There was another matter, though, which she wanted to discuss with Brooke—the pitiful shed at the back of the stable which was now Gabriela's home.

'You must work up more enthusiasm than that,' he now scolded her. 'It's a ceremony.'

'All right. What time?'

'Let's make it a quarter to twelve, say. I can see you're not going to be in a festive mood, so you can make your visit as brief as you like.'

'I'll tell Julie and Paul.'

'Tomorrow it's my turn to provide a dinner, so I've booked for the four of us at the Marroqui. That suit you?'

'Supposing I say I prefer cheese and a crust of bread at home?' she countered.

'I shouldn't believe you. Besides, you want to see the goings-on in Albarosa, don't you?'

She smiled. 'I suppose you want me to take notes for you?'

'Not this time. I can do my own note-taking.'

'I'll come if it's only to make the numbers even.'

She did not see either Paul or Julie during the rest of the day, so she assumed that they knew of the midnight rendezvous tonight. During the evening she prepared a simple meal, read for a short while and discovered that she could not keep her glance from straying constantly to her watch. Only eleven? Too soon. At half-past eleven she put a coat around her shoulders, took a torch and set off through the dark, whispering gardens. Before she was halfway, the flickering light of another torch danced before her.

'Good girl! I was just coming to call for you,' said Brooke.

In his villa there was no sign of Julie or Paul. Caran mildly wondered what Brooke was up to and, indeed, if Paul or Don Ramiro had invited her in this way and she found herself the sole guest, she might have been more apprehensive. As to Brooke, she could have few scruples since it was Julie, not herself, whom he evidently wished to capture.

His table was littered with papers and books as usual, but in a cleared space he had set a bunch of grapes on a plate and beside it two saucers each with twelve grapes.

'Julie and Paul not coming?' she asked, noting that there were only two saucers.

He shrugged indifference. 'Now you have to look slippy to keep in time with the strokes of twelve midnight. On each stroke you eat a grape.'

'What's the meaning of it?'

'To ensure good luck during the next twelve months, of course.' He switched on a transistor radio. 'Listen!' he said, glancing at his watch. 'Any moment now.'

The first 'dong' caught her unawares and she had to stuff two grapes into her mouth for the second stroke. Now she and Brooke both had the rhythm, but when he suddenly popped one of his grapes into her mouth and invited her to reciprocate, she lost count and began to laugh.

'Be serious!' he ordered, his mouth full of grapes.

By the time the last stroke sounded they were both laughing helplessly, their cheeks bulging with grapes as though with bull's-eyes.

'I need practice,' gasped Caran as she swallowed the last of her quota.

Brooke moved to the window-sill and poured two glasses of *manzanilla*. 'Happy New Year!' He raised his glass. She echoed his words and sipped her wine.

He put down his glass and came towards her, when a violent knocking on the outer door sent him to open it.

'Really, Brooke!' came Julie's voice, shrill and indignant. 'We've been waiting for ages——' She broke off when she caught sight of Caran. 'Oh! You seem to have had the correct information. Paul and I have been wasting our time in his villa.'

'Sorry about that!'

Caran was amazed at the cool, sardonic note in Brooke's voice.

'You distinctly told us to eat these blessed grapes in Paul's place,' continued Julie hotly. 'Now I suppose it's too late.'

'Wait another year, Julie,' said Brooke in a wholly different voice, silky and smooth. 'You don't really believe that a dozen grapes can influence your luck for a whole year, do you?'

'Of course it can't,' put in Paul.

Brooke poured more wine and offered it to the other two.

Julie tossed hers off with a barely audible mumble of 'Happy New Year'. She sat down in one of the vacant chairs while Paul perched on the edge of a small table.

After a few minutes of desultory conversation Caran sensed the hostile atmosphere.

'I've seen the New Year in,' she remarked casually, 'so I shall go home. Thanks for the grapes, Brooke.'

Paul immediately offered to accompany her through the darkness, but Julie remained where she was, swinging one elegant leg across the other. 'I'll stay,' she said. 'I've something to discuss with Brooke.'

Caran and Paul hastily removed themselves. Julie could not have made it plainer that she intended to give Brooke a large piece of her mind.

'I really do wish you'd accepted Don Ramiro's invitation,' complained Paul as they walked through the garden.

'A long way to go for about one minute's ceremony,' she replied smoothly.

'Oh, you know perfectly well there was more to it than that,' he said testily.

'Not as far as Brooke's concerned. We ate the grapes, drank the wine and that was all.'

She would not allow herself to think of that movement he had made towards her, his arms raised a little as if to embrace her. Had that really been his intention? Or just a chaste New Year kiss? A pity that Julie and Paul had not arrived five minutes later. She would have known then Brooke's treacherous purpose, for she suspected that his idea might be to play one girl off against the other, so that he did not become too deeply involved with either.

By now she and Paul had arrived at her villa. 'Good night, Paul,' she said quietly. 'Don't be too depressed about Julie.'

'I don't know what she sees in that fellow Eldridge,' he grumbled.

'He's rather different from the more usual type she meets. At home she wouldn't look twice at him, but here in Spain, he's a kind of novelty.'

'Then I hope the shine wears off him pretty quickly. Can't be too soon for me. Good night, Caran. Bless you.'

Caran feared that Brooke's dinner party at the Marroqui would prove a complete flop, for Julie was sulky or sarcastic by turns, Paul gloomy except when Julie threw him a kind word, but Brooke maintained a lively conversation apparently quite oblivious of any hostile undercurrents. He related some of his experiences in various parts of Spain, spoke of villages off the beaten track where old customs still existed.

'When we've finished eating here, we'll go out into the streets and watch the children enjoying themselves with their lighted brooms.'

'At this hour?' queried Carán. 'So late?'

'It's the one day of the year when they can stay up until long past midnight,' Brooke replied.

In the streets children of all ages from about six to sixteen were running about flourishing their brooms, some of which were flaring almost dangerously while others were only smouldering.

'The idea is that the children will all fan out to the fringes of the town to drive out the old year,' explained Brooke, 'so the best place for us to see the most is up at the top.'

At first Julie was walking with Brooke up the narrow alleys and stepped streets, but then after pausing in a small square, now deserted except for a black and white cat stalking across the cobbles, Caran found herself beside Brooke, while Julie and Paul followed closely behind.

Street lighting was sparse in this district and Brooke took Caran's hand to guide her through the steep alleyways. Whether Julie and Paul were too tired to follow Caran could not be sure, but the fact was that by the time she and Brooke arrived at the summit of the town, the other two were nowhere in sight.

Caran recognised the wall where Don Ramiro had brought her that evening after dinner and showed her part of his kingdom.

In almost a complete circle below the brooms flickered like fireflies until breaks occurred, where the brooms guttered out.

'In some villages or towns the children wait until the eve of Epiphany for their sport with the brooms,' Brooke murmured. 'Then they sing carols about the Three Kings, but in Albarosa, they like to be ahead.'

'Would it be possible to see from here that part of the town where Gabriela and Felipe and their family are living in a poor little shed?' she asked quietly.

He turned sharply towards her. 'How did you know where? Who told you?'

'I discovered it by accident. If I hadn't found out the truth, I should have blamed Don Ramiro.'

'It was the best I could do for them at the time,' he snapped. 'Gabriela and Felipe were quite willing to put up with it for a week or two.'

'But why make them go at all?' she asked. 'The position wasn't so urgent as all that.'

'You tell me that now! Between the lot of you, Gabriela was fast becoming a nervous wreck. Don Ramiro wasn't interested, of course, but Paul kept nagging and you in your quiet, martyred way were almost as bad. The final straw was the day when Paul cut off their gas supply. He took away the cylinders and threatened that the next day he would cut the electricity.'

'But I didn't know about this. Why didn't Gabriela tell me? I'd have done what I could to help.'

'And what accommodation could you have found, my dear Caran?'

'At least I could have persuaded Paul not to be too drastic,' she answered with spirit.

'He wouldn't have been listening,' Brooke said incisively. 'No pleadings on your part would have made the difference. He's tougher than you think.'

Caran was silent for some time. Then she said, 'What's to

happen to Gabriela now?'

'If you'd only been more patient and less of a Paul Pry, you wouldn't have known about the stable episode. I've found them part of a house. One of my workmen told me of an address where there are three comfortable rooms vacant and next week Gabriela and her brood will be better housed.'

'Thank you, Brooke,' she murmured humbly. 'But what about furniture? They haven't enough even for sleeping. One of the children was compelled to curl up like a dog in a box.'

'I've arranged for a few bits and pieces, but if you like to add some extra comforts, I think they'd accept gifts from you. But later on—I'm not telling you the address yet. You'll go along and start interfering and criticising.'

Caran burst into indignant laughter. 'You talk as though I were an over-fussy busybody. I shall wheedle the address out of Benita.'

'Ha!' he shouted triumphantly and the echoes reverberated around the walls. 'You'll get nothing out of Benita if I tell her not to talk.'

'I wonder where the other two are,' she murmured idly after a pause. It was useless to pursue the subject of Gabriela any further.

'Need we worry about them? Here, I've something——' He rummaged in one of his pockets and handed her a small flat parcel.

'Thank you, Brooke.'

'New Year present. I hope you'll like it. I intended to give it to you last night, but the other pair arrived and then you scurried off in no time.'

She was looking down at the package in her hands, undecided whether to open it here and now. The thought uppermost in her mind was that he had given Julie a Christmas present and now belatedly deemed it advisable to give Caran a little token for New Year.

He placed his hands lightly on her shoulders and drew her towards him. As he kissed her she thought with unusual savagery, Oh, yes, kiss the nice gentleman who gives you a New Year gift. Her response was negligible, but his embrace tightened and his mouth became demanding, so that against her will she relaxed. He held her in his arms, his cheek against hers. 'I shall have to go away soon,' he whispered. 'Another job.'

Her mind leapt with shock, but she controlled her actions. So this was a night of farewell; parting gifts and goodbye kisses. For a second she wondered if he were cutting loose when a business opportunity offered because he wanted to be free from Julie.

Treat all the girls alike! That was his motto. And disappear before he became involved too closely.

'Is your new job far away?' she managed to ask, stifling the ominous tears in her voice.

'Not sure. I go where the firm sends me and where the Spanish authorities think they need my help. I shan't forget you, Caran.'

'I wonder how many girls you've said those words to,' she said with a gentle laugh.

His arms instantly loosened her. He turned slightly away from her so that he was gazing over the darkened town, pierced by sporadic lights, all that remained of the circle of brooms. 'A few. There were one or two I left with regret, but in my job I've found it wiser not to become too involved.'

Exactly, Caran thought. No one could have phrased it more correctly—or bluntly—than that.

He took out a thin cigar and lit it and in the glow of the match his face was rock-hard. What did he expect her to do now? Fall into his arms, weep on his shoulder and beg him not to go away?

She would do none of these things. She would let him see that she was entirely indifferent to his casual caresses. She would impress upon him that she hadn't taken this job in Spain in order to find a husband.

'If I'm sent to another part of Spain, will you write to me, Caran?' His quietly-spoken words interrupted her train of thought.

'I daresay I can find time to type an occasional letter, telling you of all my mishaps with the summer visitors and

Paul's progress in his development plans—or his reverses.'

'I might also like to hear of Don Ramiro's progress,' he said, 'and I don't mean hotels or swimming pools. Are you really taken with him, Caran?'

'Taken?' she echoed. 'A curious word to choose, as though he were a dress I might like to buy or a cookery recipe.'

'He has a great deal to offer.' Brooke's further words saved her the trouble of finding a judicious answer to his question.

'He's hardly likely to offer it to me,' she pointed out.

'Unpredictable things happen here in Spain, the same as everywhere else. But some marriages can become merely mergers and one partner is completely subordinated.'

'Was anyone talking of marriage?' she demanded. 'What makes you so anxious to marry me off—to a Spaniard at that?'

Vaguely she was beginning to see the drift of this extraordinary conversation. Brooke, who had shown her few favours, other than the contents of the small package she still held in her hand, now wanted to make sure that she had other masculine companionship in sight, even though he was warning her about the consequences of marrying into an aristocratic Spanish family.

Paul was evidently dismissed out of hand, and to some extent Caran was glad. She would have hated Brooke if he had suggested any closer link with Paul, whom even Benita and other girls in Albarosa viewed with distrust and distaste.

'Oh, I'm not anxious to marry you off to anyone,' he said now, leaning against the stone parapet. 'No doubt when the summer season starts, you'll have innumerable young men ousting each other for a tender glance from your—what colour are they?—hazel eyes.'

'Holiday romances!' she said scornfully. 'I shall be too busy to be able to dally in the moonlight.'

'Or even dally in the darkness—as at this moment.' He sighed, and she wondered what was the reason. Surely it was the girls who were entitled to sigh when he took his departures. 'Come along. We'd better go home.'

'The others, Julie and Paul, must think we're lost.'

'They're not worrying. I know this town better than they do and it wasn't difficult to shake them off.'

As he helped her down the steep street from the summit, she glowed a little, realising that he had deliberately isolated her from the others. But of course, only to give her the present and break the news that he was soon leaving Albarosa.

When they came to a café still open, he suggested a final coffee. She took the opportunity to undo the parcel and find out what Brooke had given her.

'Oh!' Her exclamation was one of pure delight when she saw the beautiful leather wallet and purse to match in a warm, sandy brown. Both were embossed intricately on one side with a design of a pair of flamenco dancers and on the other with a conventional pattern of stars and flowers. 'Thank you, Brooke. They're exquisite. I shall use them with great pleasure.' Momentarily she forgot her resolve to be casual and distant, and when she looked up into his face she surprised a dancing gleam in his eyes, tantalising, disquieting and thrilling all at the same time. Then the waiter brought the coffee and the moment vanished.

On the way down through the town, Brooke tucked her hand into the crook of his elbow, and she thought what a pity it was that his determination not to be entrapped prevented what might develop into a pleasant friendship. Caran would have been glad to give him her unstinted and harmonious fellowship if she could have been sure that he would not mistake it for an unintended infatuation.

All the villas were in darkness, so either Paul and Julie had both returned and gone to bed or they were still enjoying themselves in the town.

At Caran's door, Brooke pressed her hand, brushed his lips against hers and murmured *'Adios!'* He muttered another word and it seemed to her fanciful hearing that he had said *'amada'*.

A breeze rustled faintly among the magnolias and oleanders, and Caran wished desperately that scientists who assert that sound waves persist could invent some method of catching the echoes.

As she entered the villa she asked herself what difference did it make if he had called her 'darling'? A casual term of endearment lightly bestowed. She would be a fool, ten times a fool, if because of one intimate evening and a handsome gift, she took his attentions seriously.

Not, of course, that she wanted to, for she was certainly not in love with him and counted herself fortunate that she could say so. Yet already the coming year seemed a trifle dimmed if Brooke left the Villa Zafiro.

CHAPTER EIGHT

CARAN did not mention Brooke's probable departure to anyone, but Paul came in one morning with the news that
Brooke was leaving his villa at the end of the month.

'I'm pleased as punch about that,' he said enthusiastically.
'He's been a pain in the neck for a long time.'

'I don't know what progress he's made with painting the
interior,' remarked Caran, 'but he did the outside.'

'Oh, as soon as he's out, we'll go to work on the villa.'
Paul was busy with jotting down notes of work to be done.

Julie's reaction was more surprising. At first she feigned
prior knowledge. 'Oh, yes, he did mention something about
leaving,' she said indifferently. A few days later she was
giggling about Brooke's attitude to women.

'Sisters in adversity, that's what we are,' she declared to
Caran one morning.

'Why? What is our shared sorrow?'

'Be yourself, Caran. You know quite well that the subject
of our joint heartache is Brooke.'

'My heart isn't aching over him,' Caran asserted stoutly.
'Is yours?'

Julie laughed joyously and this time without any derisive
note. 'Of course. So is yours, if you'd only tell the truth.
Girls like us are doomed to be left in the lurch by men who
roam about Spain or any other country. Confess, pet, that
you fell for him a little.'

Caran opened her mouth to utter a firm denial. Then she,
too, laughed. 'All right, yes. Let's say I *began* to like him,
but I didn't fall very far.'

'He isn't really good husband-material,' was Julie's sage
verdict. She perched on the arm of a chair. 'Now that I've
decided to stay here quite a long time, I shall see what I can
do for myself in the shape of a long-pursed tourist, American
for preference.'

'Oh, Julie, you're incorrigible!' Caran laughed happily.

She was glad that relations between herself and Julie had returned to a more amicable footing. 'If there's any class of people overburdened with the love-'em-and-leave-'em complex, it's tourists, American or otherwise. How many times have you warned me against the snares of soft music, moonlight and a dreamy garden full of sweet perfumes?'

'Well, it *has* been known for people to marry partners they discovered on holiday,' Julie retorted. 'So wait and see.'

'And in the meantime, what about Paul?' queried Caran.

'He understands the position only too well. He's not in love with me and, for his part, he might also meet some luscious beauty who comes here for a fortnight and stays a lifetime.'

Caran saw Brooke only a couple of times during the next three weeks, then only for a brief moment in the gardens or on the way to his car. She wondered if he had visited any further festivals in the neighbourhood and was actually a trifle piqued that he had not asked her to accompany him to any of the Epiphany fiestas. She knew that many towns and villages celebrated the Three Kings with all kinds of merrymaking.

On the other hand, he might have been compelled to spend all his time at the irrigation site supervising the repairs to the damaged roadway.

One day, however, she came upon him as he and Felipe were packing boxes and bundles of papers into a hand-cart, similar to the one that Felipe used for deliveries of groceries.

'Moving day?' she enquired of the two men.

'Not quite,' replied Brooke. 'I have to clear out all these stacks of documents and papers and get them to my next place of toil.'

'I hope it's not too far for you both,' she commented slyly. 'Hard work trundling Felipe's hand-cart over the sierras.'

'Numbskull!' he retorted. 'Hang around long enough and all will be clear to you! The truck is to save our legs up and down the path.'

She followed the two men as they trundled the cart to the car park to load the contents into a lorry and then she noticed that Felipe had a new vehicle, a large bright yellow box on wheels with a tricycle attached.

'Oh, this is an improvement,' she said warmly to Felipe.

'I thank the *señor* for it.' Felipe indicated Brooke.

'I made a deal with Felipe's employer,' explained Brooke in a brusque tone. 'A carpenter friend of mine would make the delivery box free of charge, but the grocery proprietor must pay to have his name painted on in handsome black letters. Then Felipe could whistle round the town in half the time, and think of the advertisement!'

'I'm glad Felipe can ride instead of pushing that thing,' she commented. She wanted to ask Felipe if he and his family were now reasonably housed, but she did not dare mention the subject in front of Brooke. She would have to find out when Brooke had gone.

When Brooke had gone! The thought was like a knell, but she pushed the unwelcome reflection aside and returned to her own tasks.

'We ought to give Brooke some sort of send-off,' suggested Julie towards the end of January. 'What about the four of us going to dinner at the Marroqui? Or, better still, a cosy little dinner here in your place. It needn't be an elaborate meal.'

Caran was dubious. It was always a prickly sort of foursome, with the two men often needling each other and Julie devoting her charm to whichever man she judged would enjoy the chance of making the other one jealous.

'I suppose we could,' she agreed at last. 'I'd better make sure exactly when he's going, before I start planning the menu.'

As it happened, the next two days were crowded with urgent tasks, including a trip to Almeria with Paul to choose curtain fabrics for the new villas and for refurbishing some of the old.

When eventually she went along to Brooke's villa, she was surprised to find Benita there sweeping and cleaning the empty rooms.

'Señor Brooke has gone?' she asked the girl.

Benita smiled. '*Si, señorita.* Yesterday.'

'Oh, I see.' Caran was dismayed.

'He said I was to give you this letter,' Benita continued.

Caran restrained her eagerness, for she wanted to snatch the envelope from the other girl's hand. A single sheet gave the address of Gabriela and Felipe Ribera. There was nothing else, not even an *Adios*.

She mustered a smile for Benita's benefit. 'I'm very glad about your sister. Is she comfortable? I must go and see her soon.' Caran was babbling words that held little meaning.

She scarcely heard Benita's replies. Then she asked with studied casualness, 'Do you know where the *señor* has gone?'

Benita nodded. 'In the mountains. Many miles from Zaragoza.'

'Thank you,' murmured Caran. Zaragoza and beyond! Her spirits sank. Was it mere chance or a definite plan that had led him from one end of Spain almost to the other?

Julie's reaction was flippant. 'So he's done a moonlight flit on both of us. Well, he certainly knows how to take his leave with a minimum of ceremony.'

Caran secretly wondered whether Julie would have dubbed as with 'a minimum of ceremony' that incident on New Year's night when she and Brooke had climbed to the summit of Albarosa and in the darkness he had kissed her with more feeling than she expected of a goodbye gesture. No doubt Julie would have looked for something more emotional.

Paul was patently glad of Brooke's departure and made no bones about it. 'A thorn in my flesh, that's what he was,' he declared emphatically. 'Every time I saw him I wanted to punch his jaw.'

Caran laughed at that. 'Are you handy with fisticuffs?'

'Enough to have wiped the smile off his face. Anyway, I'm glad to have the villa released. Otherwise I'd have given him notice soon and thrown him out. He could have found somewhere else in the town if he'd still be working in the district.'

'I suppose you'll want me to stay in Joyosa when the tenants come?' she queried.

'Oh, definitely. Julie and I will move out. I can stay at El

Catalan. They have a few rooms there. Julie—well——'

'She can always come back here,' offered Caran. 'There really is room for two. We shared a flat in London and we're accustomed to each other's ways.'

Paul seemed to be chewing over this suggestion. Finally he said, 'Well, we need not make definite arrangements yet.'

A series of handsome brochures and leaflets was being prepared to advertise the villas. Julie had posed for most of the photographs, but Caran appeared in a few with Paul. He had also made friends with an English couple living in Almeria and persuaded them to be photographed apparently enjoying the comfort of a month's holiday at a delightful villa in Albarosa.

By the end of February the two new villas were completed and ready for inspection by representatives of the tourist and letting companies. The five existing villas had already been inspected and approved, but so far no bookings had been made.

Paul was gloomy. He returned one morning from the post office and threw down on Caran's desk a bundle of mail.

'As far as I can see, not a single booking among the lot,' he complained. 'I shall have to go to London and see what I can rustle up with the tourist people.'

Caran was opening the letters and rapidly glancing at the contents. 'Here's one,' she said. 'Family of five want to book for first two weeks in April.'

'Direct or through an agency?' he queried.

'Agency.'

'Well, that's something, although it means that so far all our expensive direct advertising hasn't brought in a single booking.'

'It's early yet,' she assured him.

'Not for this part of Spain. If only there hadn't been so much delay one way and another, we'd have had the whole lot filled by now. People have discovered the benefit of winter holidays. Not everyone wants to go skiing or wintersporting in Switzerland or Norway. Two or three weeks in the sun makes a perfect break in the middle of an English winter.'

Caran began to laugh. 'Paul! You're quoting the write-up in your catalogue.'

He laughed, too. 'Am I? Well, I've lived with the blessed thing so long that I'm surprised not to be saying it over and over in my sleep.'

'One suggestion I could make. If there are any more inspections, we ought to mock up the supplies. It looks dreary to open an empty refrigerator. We could easily put in empty packets and bottles. We could stock up the bar with empty wine bottles and so on, as well as cigarette boxes. I don't think those representatives really understood how well our villas would be stocked with provisions to start off the holiday.'

Paul nodded. 'Not a bad idea, Caran.' Then he laughed. 'You better be careful, though, to take out the dummies and replace with real goods before any visitors come in. Or there'll be the devil to pay if people come in and find nothing but empties.'

'I'll take care of that,' Caran assured him. 'The show is not for the visitors, but the critical tourist people.'

'They have a right to be critical,' conceded Paul. 'They risk their own reputations for reliability and visitors who are disappointed one year never come again and make sure that their friends don't come either. We suffered for that last year. That's why I want to make this year a rattling success.'

Caran was fired with the enthusiasm of her idea and began to think of additional elaborations. A chicken in the fridge. How could that be contrived? Then she thought of Felipe and the small animals he had been making for his children. Could he make mock chickens?

She called on him the next evening. He and Gabriela had made a comfortable home out of the three rooms which Brooke had found for them over a shop which sold leather goods and crockery, men's hats and ironmongery. Caran had visited the family several times since Brooke had given her the address and been warmly welcomed. Discreetly she had been able to provide curtain material, a rug or two and some blankets for the children's beds.

Felipe listened carefully to Caran's explanations of what

she wanted. Then both he and Gabriela entered into the spirit of the idea.

'I can wash eggshells,' suggested Gabriela, 'when they are in half and you can arrange them in a rack.'

'I can make tomatoes and onions and pimentoes,' added Felipe.

In the end, the three were on the way to stuffing a whole villa with dummy representations of everything needed.

Caran noticed with pleasure how much happier this couple appeared now that they had a reasonably decent home and fewer worries. Gabriela was taking more pride in her appearance and looked quite smart in one of the dresses Caran had given her. Felipe, too, was less haggard and his eyes had lost their haunted look.

A week later Felipe came spinning down the road to the villas with his bright yellow delivery box tricycle. First he unloaded the assorted groceries ordered from the shop where he and Benita worked. Then he took out a large cardboard box and set it in the porch of Caran's villa.

'*Imitados!*' he said, laughing, then added that she had better not mix them up with the real chickens and biscuits.

He waited a few minutes while she unwrapped the packages inside. A marvellously browned chicken, half eggshells stuck firmly into a rack, carrots and onions, Felipe and Gabriela had fashioned them all.

'They're splendid!' she told him, paid him generously and ordered another couple of sets. Later in the day she found time to take the assorted items to one of the new villas and stow them in the fridge. She viewed the collection and laughed quietly. All that was needed now was a luscious-looking round of beef such as electricity showrooms use to fill up their refrigerators on show. Oh, well, she might even get Felipe on that, too.

Footsteps sounded in the living room or porch and she came out of the kitchen, imagining that one of the gardeners had seen her and wanted some instructions. Instead, Don Ramiro stood between the porch and the living room.

She gave him a greeting in a normal tone. Since Christmas he had paid a number of visits to the villas, often for long discussions with Paul, sometimes staying to a simple meal. His attitude towards Caran had not varied and now she began to believe that on that day at his house in Almeria, she must have mistaken his intentions. It was true that his dark eyes often held an amorous glint, but she attributed that to his Iberian race.

'You are busy here today?' he asked now.

'No, just finished. Come and see.' She held open the door of the fridge and he prodded the mock chicken, so brown and shining, touched the cellophane-wrapped carrots.

'They are very real,' he commented.

She locked the outer door when they left and waited for him to explain why he had followed her here.

'Are the lettings going well?' he asked.

Caran was cautious. She did not know how far she could trust Don Ramiro in business matters. 'As well as one can expect, considering how many delays we've had.'

They strolled down the sloping spit of land on which the two new villas were built. Already spring had definitely arrived here with masses of flowers, blue, yellow, mauve; the opposite shore across the narrow bay was clothed with brighter, sharper greens as the bushes sprang into leaf and the smooth sea below was emerald glass shading to smoke blue towards the horizon.

'Much could be done with this piece of land,' Don Ramiro commented.

'A large and showy hotel, a swimming pool and so on?' she queried amiably.

'More than that. A small pier or jetty, I think you call it in English, running out just there'—he pointed over the bay— 'then you could have pleasure boats from Matana or the opposite way along the coast. It would be very profitable and not make the place ugly.'

'A jetty,' she murmured, seeing distinct possibilities in the idea. Visitors always wanted to go in small boats from one place to another, especially the peripatetic English who were never satisfied to be fastened down in one place. 'I must mention it to Paul.'

'He has already heard about it. The owner of the land is

the difficulty.'

'I see. Probably in due course it can all be arranged,' she suggested confidently.

'At a high price, perhaps. If someone desires a piece of land, or even other possessions, and the seller knows that, the cost goes up accordingly.'

'Naturally,' she agreed. 'That's known as merely business principle.'

'Come, we will not waste our time discussing business transactions.' He took her hand to guide her down the rough, stony path leading to the shore and on the little headland a patch of coarse grass was inviting enough to sit on.

'I'm re-opening my villa here this week,' he told her, his face in profile as he stared out of the bay to the open sea. 'Will you come one day and see it?'

Caran laughed softly. 'That will make a nice change to inspect someone else's villa instead of the critics coming to us. But I don't really mean "inspect". I meant I shall enjoy looking at it.'

He turned swiftly to face her. 'Are you planning to stay in Spain a long time? Or is this a job you've taken for a year?'

She was surprised by his question. 'I've no definite plans either for staying or going home,' she said slowly. 'But, apart from perhaps a short visit to my parents in England, I hope to stay here quite a long time.' Now that Brooke had gone to the other end of Spain, she could view with more tranquillity the prospect of staying at Albarosa indefinitely, as long as her job and conditions were mutually satisfactory.

'Managing the villas?' he queried.

She nodded. 'I suppose so. Paul has certain plans for development and expansion, so there should be something here that I can do.'

He gave her a slow smile and his dark eyes gleamed. 'I think it is not the kind of post for you. You are wasted on trivialities—like stocking up refrigerators.'

'That was only window-dressing.' She rose to her feet. 'That reminds me that I have work to do.'

'As you wish, although I think your tasks are not important. I was about to suggest that we might go into the town for lunch. Then you can busy yourself this afternoon with your typing and so on.'

Caran hesitated. A brusque refusal would not cost her more than an expensive lunch, but Paul's delicate business arrangements might possibly suffer a setback.

She was really in the dark as to the business understanding between him and Don Ramiro, uncertain whether it was a matter of rivalry or collaboration. Yet it was difficult to imagine Don Ramiro being concerned in commercial development schemes. He was reputedly rich enough already.

She decided to accept his invitation now. 'But I mustn't have too prolonged a lunch hour,' she warned him.

On the way to his car parked behind the villas, Caran met Benita, who gave her a smiling *'Buenos dias!'*

'So I was wrong about your helping that girl's family to better housing,' she said.

'What family was that?' he asked vaguely.

With a measure of impatience she related the happenings concerning Gabriela and Felipe, stressing that Brooke Eldridge had been entirely responsible for helping them.

Don Ramiro shrugged. 'If I had known how near to your heart such a plan was, I would have done all I could to find them a dwelling.'

As she entered his car she gave him an oblique glance which he could interpret how he liked. For her part, she was not taken in by his flowery phrases.

After the leisurely lunch she was surprised when instead of driving her back to the villas he took the serpentine road that led out of the town towards Almeria.

'You can spare time for a brief visit to my villa?'

Short of flinging herself out of the car on to the precipitous track and rolling down the hillside, she could scarcely refuse. Fortunately the distance was not far and he soon arrived at a pair of white gates opened after a few minutes by an old man evidently summoned by a horn, after Don Ramiro had ineffectually jangled a large bell.

The Villa Mendosa was actually a large country house with Moorish arches, several courtyards and patios, many already filled with tubs and vast pots of flowers.

The balconies, supported by black twisted pillars or winged horses, were almost obscured by masses of wistaria.

Little ornamental fountains remained silent over their half-empty pools, but indicated where, later on, they would murmur softly in drops of sparkling light.

Inside the house the entrance hall seemed dark by contrast with the sunlight outside, but Don Ramiro led Caran through various rooms into a magnificent drawing room with tall double windows all along one side.

'This is particularly what I wished to show you.'

She followed him to the windows. Over a sloping garden was a view of the sea, almost dark purple today, a rocky headland and, beyond, the wide sweeping curve of Albarosa's shore line.

'It will amuse you, perhaps,' he said, 'to find that before the cult of sea and sun, our predecessors built their houses with their backs to the sea. In fact, some of our neighbours were slightly ashamed of having the sea in view at all.'

'Different now,' commented Caran. 'Anyone will pay a high price for sea views.'

'My father had this room constructed out of what were servants' quarters, store-rooms and such. We have made them a new wing at the side.'

'A handsome room,' Caran agreed, noting the carved cornices above the arched windows, the turquoise brocade walls and the soft blend of grey and rose in the carpet.

'But of course it is a woman's room, you understand,' said Don Ramiro, glancing at her.

'A woman's room?' she echoed.

'It is very feminine. Indeed, my father really had it arranged for my mother and her friends.'

She smiled at him. 'You mean that Spanish men prefer the austerity of dark wood furniture and leather walls?'

'Perhaps so. Our family *casa* in Almeria is like that, although there are pleasant little rooms for the women.'

She wondered why he was telling her all this.

'But come with me and I will show you the rest of the villa.'

He conducted her on a tour of several rooms on the ground floor, some of them with the furniture still dust-sheeted.

'The servants have only just begun to put the place in order for me,' he explained. 'In a week or so, everything will be comfortable and arranged properly—even with flowers in the vases.' He gave her a warm smile at the last words.

Upstairs there were bedrooms, some with dark rosewood furniture and massive wardrobes with intricate carvings, others in pale woods or white painted suites.

Caran suppressed the desire to liken Don Ramiro to a house agent showing a property to a prospective customer. She was complimentary about everything, because she imagined that was what he expected.

Then he returned to the elegant drawing room and when she approached the windows for another glance at the view, he took her hands in his own.

'All this—and everything else that I own—all can be yours, Caran,' he said quietly.

For the moment she was stunned.

'I wish to marry you,' he said almost without emotion.

'But—I'm English——' she stammered.

'Does that matter? Does it matter to you that I am Spanish?'

'But your family? They'll expect you to marry someone of your own nationality.'

'My father is dead and I am now head of the family. My mother wishes only to see me happy. She does not yet know you, but she approves that you might be a good choice.'

'But, Don Ramiro, you, too, know very little of me. In England my parents are simple folk, not at all rich nor aristocratic.'

'That is not important. I am wealthy enough not to worry about money.' He smiled suddenly. 'As for aristocratic birth, my great-grandfather married a peasant girl from Murcia. She could neither read nor write, she walked barefoot until he bought shoes for her, and with his help she became an illustrious member of our house.'

At least, thought Caran, Don Ramiro wouldn't have to teach her to read or write, and she was in the habit of wearing shoes!

She shook her head slowly. 'No, Don Ramiro, it would

not be for the happiness of either of us, but I appreciate the honour you have done me.'

'Is there someone else? You have a fiancé in England? Or——'

'No, I've no one in England,' she assured him.

'Or the Englishman here? He who works on the irrigation? Tell me that you are not bound to him!'

'Oh, no, indeed.' Caran could truthfully answer that. Brooke had left her free as the air. 'He has gone to Zaragoza, I believe, or somewhere in that direction.'

'Then there is no obstacle,' he said confidently. 'Now I will take you back to your villa and you will consider my offer. I am aware that all girls like to hesitate a little first before committing themselves. It would not look right for them if they said "Yes" immediately.'

Caran had the impression that although the villa seemed deserted and only in the process of being opened up for the summer, servants lurked behind doors or scurried along passages at Don Ramiro's approach.

As she left the main door she noticed the shield of the Mendosas worked in coloured mosaics on the floor, two winged horses with lances and at their feet a ship, a globe and an open book.

On the way back to her villa he was not talkative, and she was glad. To maintain a steady flow of chatter would have been out of tune with her mood and probably his.

Only when he reached the car park behind the villas did he refer to other visits. 'Paul is going to London in a day or two, so I hear. Is that so?'

'Yes. He's arranged to leave tomorrow.'

'Then perhaps you will allow me to bring you again to the villa, with your friend Julie. We shall have all the rooms straightened and all in order.'

'Could I let you know about that?' she asked. 'I shall have quite a lot of work to do in Paul's absence.'

His eyes momentarily flickered with annoyance and she realised that Don Ramiro was accustomed to his invitations being in the nature of a command, as Paul had once pointed out.

He recovered his smooth manner, smiled and raised her hand to his lips in the most courteous gesture.

Caran went through to her bedroom and flung herself on the bed. Well, of all things to happen! Señora Caran Mendosa and all that string of names to adopt. How much pushing had Paul done in this? Caran was acutely aware that in all the conversation today with Don Ramiro there had not been one word of love. He had not even said that he was fond of her. What sort of marriage would it be with a man like that?

Then, as though the room was intent on giving her back the echo, she recalled Brooke's words on New Year's night when he had taken her to the summit of Albarosa. 'He has a great deal to offer . . . some marriages can become merely mergers . . . one partner completely subordinated . . .'

Marriage with Don Ramiro was very remote from Caran's aspirations and she had treated as a joke all those little half-sentences from Paul or Brooke or Julie indicating their view that if she set out to capture Don Ramiro success would crown her efforts. Perhaps her colleagues had seen matters in a clearer, sharper light than she had realised.

Don Ramiro had graciously allowed her time for consideration of his offer, time she did not need, for even if she had never met Brooke, she knew she could not contemplate marrying this handsome Spaniard whom she had encountered on first coming to Albarosa.

At the same time she was aware that his proposal had altered her circumstances here. With Brooke far away and the prospect of never seeing him again, she would not be able to stay indefinitely at the villas. She would certainly stay as long as she could and had committed herself to the approaching summer season. After that she would have to make new plans to suit whatever conditions were present then.

For the first time she now admitted to herself that she would have felt very differently this afternoon if it had been Brooke asking her to marry him. She would not have hesitated before saying 'Yes', even if by Spanish standards that was an unseemly thing to do.

CHAPTER NINE

CARAN was undecided whether to tell Julie of Don Ramiro's offer. Then it occurred to her that Don Ramiro might easily call or telephone and in Caran's absence Julie might accept invitations to the Villa Mendosa for both of them.

Julie's reaction was surprised satisfaction. 'What a success story!' She hugged Caran and kissed her. 'Actually, I never thought you'd pull it off.'

'Wait a minute and listen. I haven't accepted him.'

'What! But you can't turn down an offer from an aristocrat like that. You're out of your mind.'

'Not in the least,' retorted Caran. 'I'm not going to change my mind, either. It's "No" and it's going to stay "No". It would be all wrong. I'd be swamped with tradition and ceremony. I'd be a stranger in the house, all his houses.'

'You're thinking of all his delightful womenfolk, his mother and those cousins—especially that charming Mirella. But you've enough spirit to stand up to them, surely.'

'I'm not sure that I have,' admitted Caran. 'If you're so cocksure about it all, why don't you marry him instead?'

Julie laughed delightedly. 'You haven't forgotten that you're the one he's asked, not me?'

'If you set out to win him, you'd succeed. You always do.'

Julie was silent for a moment or two. Then she said more seriously, 'You're not letting ideas about Brooke stand in your way, are you?'

'Brooke? Of course not.' Caran's denial was too swift and she knew it, for her cheeks flushed. She turned her face away so that Julie should not see that tell-tale sign. 'Brooke goes where the job goes and picks up his girls as though they were dolls in a shop. Just as easy to put down again.' She tried to keep out the slightly bitter edge to her voice.

'Well, I won't let you in for further visits, at least while Paul's away,' Julie promised. 'I really don't fancy myself in the role of *duenna*. Do you think he has one of those three-seater affairs shaped like a shamrock? I don't know the proper name, but the lovers sit adjacent in their separate seats and the chaperone in the third. Very useful to put out a restraining hand when the embraces become too close.'

Caran laughed. 'I'm not going to ask Don Ramiro for your special benefit.'

'How old do you think he is?' asked Julie.

'Don Ramiro? Oh, about thirty or so, I should think. He hasn't told me,' Caran giggled.

'He's nearer thirty-five, I should guess. Why hasn't he married before now, I wonder?'

'Been turned down by a succession of heartless English and other foreign girls, perhaps,' suggested Caran.

'Callous, that's what you are, pet,' was Julie's equally unfeeling comment.

Paul was away for just over a week and brought his aunt, Mrs. Parmenter, back with him. He had arranged before his departure that she was to have the Villa Cristal, where Gabriela had once lived. 'Then we shall really find out if the place has been left in good order everywhere,' he said.

Caran was unimpressed with this pseudo-logic, for the whole villa had been thoroughly overhauled and redecorated since Gabriela and Felipe had left.

She was glad to welcome the woman who was actually her employer, and keen to show all the improvements that had been made.

'You've done very well indeed,' Mrs. Parmenter complimented her.

'Not alone, though,' objected Caran. 'Paul has done a great deal himself.'

'I'm sure we shall have a good season. Paul called on various travel agencies in London and we have a number of provisional bookings and some firm ones.'

'Good. I don't really feel that I've justified my job as manager until we have all the villas occupied.'

Mrs. Parmenter gave Caran a strange look, but smiled the next moment. 'I knew you would be very conscientious.'

For several evenings Paul accompanied his aunt and the

two girls to dinner at El Catalan or the Marroqui, and Caran was glad to be relieved of the necessity of cooking meals in her villa. One evening Julie had driven to Almeria earlier to check on some printing of leaflets that was being done there and Paul said, 'No use waiting for Julie. She won't be back until fairly late.'

At the Marroqui Caran was trying to enjoy the present moment and not remember the other occasions when she had been here with Don Ramiro or Brooke.

'A lot of credit is due to Caran,' Paul was saying. 'We might not have pulled it off if she hadn't worked so hard.'

Caran turned towards the other two. 'What hard work have I done?' she asked.

Paul did not reply, for he was ordering champagne from the waiter, but Mrs. Parmenter said eagerly, 'You've enabled us to sell the villas at a handsome profit.'

'Sell? But—I don't understand——'

'We've brought off a marvellous deal with Don Ramiro,' explained Paul. 'You remember I showed you some plans for development of the neck of land by the shore?'

She nodded, for she had no adequate words.

'Well, the trouble was that Don Ramiro also wanted to come in on developing Albarosa into a first-class resort. A year ago he bought the piece of land on which our villas stand. He owns all the rest on either side, but that little plot belonged to someone else.'

'Then it was only a change of ownership. You told me you only rented the land,' Caran pointed out. She seemed to be lost in a fog.

'Yes, but Don Ramiro wants to develop the whole place as a complete village—hotels, shops, a jetty for boats, the lot.'

Caran remembered that reference to a small pier.

'And our villas are in the way,' added Mrs. Parmenter happily.

'So we've extracted really handsome compensation for them,' continued Paul. 'Now you see why I wanted everything to be in first-class condition. Also, I wanted compensation for the loss of lettings, next year and several years after that. Aunt Alison deserves to be properly reimbursed not only for the money she's spent on the places, but also for the loss of income in the future.'

Caran felt choked. 'Do you mean that the villas are to be pulled down, swept away to make room for something else?' she asked in a painfully constricted voice.

'That's right,' agreed Paul, smiling. 'But wait a year and you'll see what will rise in their place.'

'Why bother to have finished the two new villas if they're going to be demolished?' she demanded.

'Because that way we get reimbursed for two completed villas, instead of half-built affairs.'

'I think Paul has managed the whole affair quite splendidly,' asserted his aunt, giving him an admiring glance.

'I couldn't have done it half as well without Caran's help,' he countered modestly. 'You excelled yourself, Caran, by knowing just how much to encourage Don Ramiro, then withdrawing. You played your cards like an expert.'

Caran instantly recalled that other occasion on the way back from the visit to Don Ramiro in Almeria when Paul had remarked to Julie that Caran knew how to play her cards.

Now she said with flat bitterness, 'Apparently I've played them so well that Don Ramiro has asked me to marry him.'

'What!' Paul's hand holding his glass shook so violently that some of the champagne spilled on the table. 'Why, that's marvellous news. Congratulations! Oh, we shall have to drink a separate toast to that!' He was already signalling to the waiter for more champagne.

'You'd better wait before you order,' Caran said quietly. 'I'm not going to accept Don Ramiro.'

Paul's pent-up breath came out in a huge gasp. 'Not accept him? You're crazy! Remember how I told you ages ago that he'd really fallen for you and you wouldn't believe me? I said then that if you wanted to, you could end up by being a Mendosa.'

'As it happens, I don't want to end up that way.'

After a long pause, during which Caran noticed that Mrs. Parmenter remained silent and unsmiling, Paul said sadly, 'Well, you can't be compelled to change your mind, but I hope you'll give yourself time to think it over. Chance in a million.'

'I'm aware of that,' agreed Caran with a faint smile. 'Aristocratic Dons aren't lying around waiting for me to give them my gracious favours.'

'Why, you even managed to get Brooke Eldridge out of the way,' Paul continued. 'He soon hopped it when he saw that he had no chance with you—or Julie, either, for that matter.'

'I don't think he went because of any personal reasons.' Caran kept her voice steady. 'It was merely because of a job elsewhere.'

'Anyway, his villa is empty, so it saves me the necessity of turning him out.'

He poured more champagne. 'Let's at least drink a toast to our new venture—the Hotel Peninsula. Remember, Caran, you christened it?'

She shook her head. 'No, Paul. You did.'

He filled her glass and she held it near her lips so that the bubbles gently spattered her face, but she did not drink. She would have preferred to fling the contents into Paul's face, and perhaps to a lesser degree, Mrs. Parmenter's.

'Of course, Caran,' began Paul, 'even if you don't choose to marry Don Ramiro, you'll still be in clover. We'll make you a director and the rewards will be handsome. If you want to occupy your time, you'll have a free hand to dabble in anything you choose, interior decoration, supervising the sales—we shall have all kinds of boutiques in the hotel and elsewhere.'

Paul's enthusiasm ran on into a brilliant future. Caran reflected that she was asking too much if she expected him to be sensitive over her disappointment. He was not made that way. He saw his objective and drove straight towards it, thrusting sentiment or the misfortunes of others aside without a qualm.

When Paul drove her and Mrs. Parmenter back to the villas, he said, 'Come into mine, Caran, and I'll show you all the plans.'

'Not tonight, Paul. I'm rather tired. You can show them

to me another time.'

He accepted her refusal, but his aunt had another purpose in view.

'Would you come into Cristal for a few moments?' she asked Caran, and it was useless refusing that request.

Paul saw them to the outer door of Cristal and bade them good night.

'You're upset about our future plans, aren't you?' Mrs. Parmenter began when she and Caran were in the living-room of the villa.

'I've no right to be, I suppose,' Caran answered, 'but I think you should have told me when you engaged me that you intended to put the villas into working order and then sell them.'

She wanted to say that Mrs. Parmenter and Paul had encouraged her to accept a post under completely false pretences and then used her as a pawn in the game of bargaining with Don Ramiro.

'But at that time we had no intention of doing that,' Mrs. Parmenter now asserted. 'I'd lost money in previous years through bad management and my only idea was to have someone trustworthy on the spot. It was Paul who had ideas about development, but only after you had already left England.'

'Oh, I thought he spoke as though such ideas had been in his mind a considerable time, more than a year, in fact.' Caran was not to be coaxed so easily.

'In a vague way, yes,' admitted the other woman. 'But what really sparked him off was the fact that you'd met Don Ramiro before Paul came. Then he discovered that Don Ramiro had bought the land here and was virtually our new landlord. Paul soon saw that he had to work fast to make the villas an attractive proposition.'

It was all very plausible, Caran thought. So Don Ramiro had been involved from her first day in Spain. She saw now, or perhaps imagined she saw, why the mere mention of the villas was enough to make people in Albarosa shake their heads. The bills not paid, the refusal of maids to give service, the reluctance of builders and others to do the repairs, all these hindrances were no doubt contrived by the most influential man in the neighbourhood, Don Ramiro. If the villas failed, he would be able to buy them at knockout price.

Instead of that, Caran had been subtly persuaded to put in a certain amount of hard work and a great deal of enthusiasm, with the result that the villas were worthy of greater compensation.

'I was quite surprised at your news about Don Ramiro,' Mrs. Parmenter broke in on Caran's thoughts. 'Of course, it would be a tremendous chance for you to marry him, although I believe that it's not always easy to be integrated into one of these proud Spanish families.'

'You need not worry about that, Mrs. Parmenter. I shan't marry Don Ramiro.'

Mrs. Parmenter's face brightened. 'In one way I'm glad to hear that, and obviously you have your reasons.' She looked away from Caran, then back again quickly. 'I've had the idea lately that you and Paul would make a splendid pair.'

'Paul—and me?' echoed Caran. Belatedly she schooled her face into a less appalled expression. 'Oh, no, that wouldn't please either of us.'

'I like you very much, Caran, not because you've worked well here, but because of your good qualities in a personal way. You'd be very good for Paul, have a steadying influence on him. He's a dear nephew, but inclined quite often to be attracted to the wrong girl.'

Caran smiled gently. 'He's not attracted to me.' It was on the tip of her tongue to add that if he were attracted to anyone here, Julie was the girl.

'That may be, but I can see that he's attracted to your friend Julie.' Mrs. Parmenter took the words straight out of Caran's thoughts. 'Now I don't want to be harsh and she's your friend, but she isn't at all suitable for Paul.'

'She has a good business head,' put in Caran in Julie's defence.

'Too good, perhaps, in some directions. That girl is out to make a successful financial match and she sees a comfortable future in Paul.'

'I think you're wrong, Mrs. Parmenter. Julie has quite other ideas.'

'Then in that case she's leading Paul on for no purpose,' was the other's crisp reply. 'Well, for the time being we shall have to allow matters to settle themselves, I suppose. One thing I'm glad of, and that's getting rid of Mr. Eldridge. I know his rent was useful when all the other villas were empty, but he was so untidy and gave a bad, shabby air to the whole place.'

Caran laughed. 'He won't trouble you again. He's gone to the opposite end of Spain on another irrigation scheme.' She rose to go, for evidently Mrs. Parmenter's little chat was finished.

'You will stay on with us whatever happens, won't you, Caran?' queried Mrs. Parmenter.

'I shan't leave you in mid-season,' Caran declared coldly. 'I was engaged to manage the villas during this coming summer and unless you have other plans, I shall do so. Paul says there are bookings running into September, so I take it that the villas won't be knocked down until after then.'

Mrs. Parmenter smiled. 'No question of demolition for a long time yet, not until the hotel is built and occupied, and that will be well into next year. So I hope we shall keep you here for some time.'

With that reassurance Caran said good night to Mrs. Parmenter and returned to her villa. The savour had gone out of the whole project now. Paul and his aunt might be delighted at events to come, but Caran was depressed. If only Brooke had been here to talk to, to tell him of her disappointment, she would have borne with good humour his sarcastic remarks.

Julie was sympathetic when the two girls met next day.

'You're upset about all the business deal, aren't you? Don't worry. It will sort itself out. That's what I say about slogging in a job, any job. You give out your heart's blood to do more than you need and what happens? Your employers say "Oh, thanks very much" and you find yourself looking for a new job, for one reason or another.'

In spite of her depression, Caran laughed at Julie's philosophy. 'These people are your employers, too.'

'Yes, but I summed up Paul long ago. As for his auntie, she's one of those helpless middle-aged women who need half a dozen friends or relatives to keep them from sinking under the weight of their bad investments, but actually, they're tough as old boots and end up frightfully rich, leaving someone else to pay the death duties.'

At that Caran laughed without restraint. 'Dear Julie, you really are a tonic when I feel low. Aunt Alison wouldn't be flattered by your opinion of her.'

'And you needn't tell me her opinion of me. I know what she thinks. That I'm out to grab her darling Paul. Well, you know, Caran, what I think about him. As for you, my pet, if matters really get you down, you can always marry the Don. I'm off to the town. Anything you want?'

'Yes. Will you bring a few packets of assorted sewing needles and some reels of thread? Black and white, half a dozen of each. I thought I'd make up small boxes of mending materials for the villas. People often forget to bring such items with them and they don't know enough Spanish to ask in the shops.'

Julie stood, arms akimbo, and gave Caran a long, admiring glance. 'You never really stop working, do you? In spite of a clout over the head.'

'It passes the time,' murmured Caran, smiling. She opened her wallet and gave Julie a five-hundred-peseta note.

'That's a handsome wallet you have there,' commented Julie. 'Did you buy it here?'

Caran coloured furiously. 'No. It was a present. New Year.'

Julie took it from Caran's hands and examined the designs on back and front. 'H'm. I remember that Paul gave you perfume. Don Ramiro would never compromise himself in the matter of gifts before engagement, so who could it be but Brooke?'

Caran nodded. 'Just a farewell trifle, that's all,' she said offhandedly, as she took it back from Julie.

'A token of his regard. You fared better than I did. That necklace—the amber beads—that wasn't from Brooke. I bought it myself.'

'You—bought it?'

'Thought it might make you jealous. 'Bye!' Julie dashed along the path to the road.

Caran leaned against the door lintel. The more I know of Julie, she thought, the more astonishing I find her. Was it true that she had brought her own necklace and pretended it was a gift from Brooke? Or was she just saying that now that she knew Caran had also received a present? Caran was conscious of a tiny glow of warmth towards Brooke. But the spark soon died. Why imagine that he had been drawn towards her, even in preference to Julie, when he was now so far away and unlikely to be sparing her a single tender thought?

Three days before Good Friday, Caran received a letter from Don Ramiro inviting her to attend the processions and ceremonies on that day in Granada.

Without hesitation Caran replied, regretfully declining on the grounds that the first visitors to the villas would be arriving just before Easter and she would be extra busy.

She knew quite well that if she accepted, Don Ramiro would interpret her acceptance into at least a provisional acceptance of his offer of marriage. She would be seen in Granada in his company in public and that would designate her as his intended bride.

Paul apparently knew of this invitation, for he told Caran that she could take a day or two off.

'I suppose Don Ramiro will come and pick you up to drive you to Granada?'

Caran gave him a cautious glance. 'I'm not going to Granada,' she said quietly.

'Oh, that's bad news! Why not?'

'You of all people, Paul, ought to know why not. If I go, it's tantamount to saying that I'll marry the man—some time.'

Paul sighed. 'It means a lot to us, Caran, not to offend him. Perhaps you'll change your mind?'

'No, I think not. Besides, we have people coming in on

Thursday. I ought to be here to settle them in.'

'Aunt Alison and I will do everything that's necessary for the visitors,' he promised eagerly.

But Caran was not to be swayed. She would stick to her resolve not to go to Granada. It was a pity, she thought, to miss such an interesting spectacle in Holy Week. Apart from that, she would have liked to visit Granada to see the Alhambra and the gardens of the Generalife, but perhaps later on she would be able to do that.

On Thursday morning there was a peremptory knock on the outer door and she rushed to open it, thinking that Felipe had brought some more of his clay dummies for display. Instead, Brooke stood there, smiling, unwontedly tidy in jacket and cavalry twill trousers.

'Happy Maundy Thursday!' he greeted her. He stepped inside with as little ceremony as if he were still living at his villa and had come to bring her the morning paper.

'Oh, hallo, Brooke!' she muttered fatuously, annoyed with herself that he should have the power to throw her off balance. 'On holiday?'

'Yes. Too difficult to get the men to work during this week. They're all involved in various processions and then the Easter gaieties. So I've taken some time off myself. How about you? Any time to spare?'

She shook her head. 'Not a hope. We have our first visitors coming today.'

'Pity. Thought I'd like to see the Good Friday turn-out at Murcia. I couldn't see it last year because I went to Lorca for theirs. No chance of coming with me—if only to take shorthand notes?'

She was tempted and he knew it, but did he think he could just march in and invite her to a day's outing when two months ago he had left his villa without a word, without even telling her to what district he was moving, let alone trust her with his address?

'Sorry,' she murmured, 'but I've already refused one invitation.'

The moment she had spoken she realised she had made a mistake. Never tell one man that you have already turned

166

down another's offer, Julie had once counselled her. It merely makes the second one keener to overcome your opposition and score off his rival.

'All the more reason for coming with me,' said Brooke, seizing his advantage as she knew he would. Yet one part of her mind rejoiced that he was taking the trouble to persuade her.

But she would not surrender quite so easily. 'I'll have to let you know later,' she temporised.

'How late? This afternoon when you've squared it with Paul? We have to leave at seven tomorrow morning if we're to arrive in Murcia in time to see the important parts of the processions.'

She recovered her poise and some of her spirit. 'You never think of anyone but yourself and your festivals, do you? Here am I trying to put on a good show and create an excellent impression for the tourists and you barge in with offers of a day's secretarial work in Murcia!'

Brooke's raised eyebrows looked comic. 'You could do with a day off from the grind here. You look peaky.'

'I've worked here all the winter, even though it wasn't very hard, and now I'm looking forward to the summer. If I don't have too many interruptions, I might even have a chance to get tanned.'

Brooke pushed his hands into his jacket pockets and laughed rudely. 'Flying off the handle as usual. Ah! Summer at Albarosa. A fine prospect. I wish I could be here to enjoy it.'

'I should never get any work done then.'

'Who would be interrupting you? Not I. All right then, I'll take myself off—I'd have given you lunch in the town if you'd been in a more gracious mood. I shall take Benita instead.'

'Do. She'll enjoy a good meal.'

'I'll be in the car park tomorrow morning. If you're not there sharp on seven, I shall go without you.'

'Taking Benita there?' she queried impudently.

'Oh, I've the pick of the girls in this town.' He went out without another word and a few moments later she heard the

167

sound of his car behind the villas, then roaring up the winding road.

Caran stood for a moment or two in the porch, dazed by the unexpectedness of Brooke's visit. Had he really come specially to invite her to a fiesta at Murcia or because he had a few days to fill in and was at a loose end? Going to fiestas and ceremonies on his own was too dull for words. One might as well have the company of a girl. Any girl? She could almost imagine the way his mind worked. She was still uncertain whether to go or not.

The rest of the day was spent in settling in the party of six. Paul had moved into Brooke's former Villa Zafiro, leaving Turquesa, next door to Caran, free for this party. In due course he would lodge at El Catalan, Julie would vacate Esmeralda and come back to Caran's, Joyosa.

The family expressed themselves delighted with everything and relieved to find that an English girl was in charge and they were not expected to speak Spanish. There were two middle-aged couples accompanied by a pair of teenage daughters who might belong to either parents, since the whole lot shared the same surname, so were obviously related.

'The maid Elena will work for you six hours each day,' Caran explained. 'Usually our girls work three or four hours, say ten till two, and the rest of the time in the evening seven till nine, perhaps, but if you want alterations, we can arrange that. If you will give Elena your shopping requirements each evening, she will usually order or bring with her food for the day. Please tell her if you want to be away in the middle of the day.'

Caran congratulated herself and Julie that the latter had eventually secured the services of one maid with the promise of four or five more. So that was one worry less.

Julie was spending the weekend in Malaga with some new acquaintances she had met and when Caran prepared herself for bed, long past midnight, she found herself secretly glad that Julie was some distance away. There would be no need of explanations if she decided to go to Murcia tomorrow.

Not that Caran had the slightest intention of doing so, she

168

told herself while setting her alarm clock for a quarter to six.

She was wearing a new coral dress of fine wool with a cream jacket and a small hat to match when she opened the door of Brooke's car next morning. A distant chime from the church in Albarosa sounded seven strokes.

'I'm glad you took me seriously about punctuality,' he observed. 'I wouldn't have waited.'

'All this creeping about in the early morning is quite ridiculous,' she said.

'Yes, that colour suits you,' he commented, starting his engine. 'At least I'm unlikely to lose you in the crush in Murcia.'

He took the coast road through Matana, then to Aguilas and Cartagena. 'It's slightly longer this way, but if we go more direct, we shall never get through Lorca with all the crowds arriving there for their fiesta.'

Since most of the district was new to Caran she did not mind which route he took. The road was bordered with aloe hedges and palm trees and sometimes through the gaps she could see a silvery canal snaking across the patchwork landscape. Here and there a square white house or a collection of several smaller ones punctuated the pattern until the scene faded into a distant line of mauve and grey-blue hills.

'You see that plain over there?' Brooke pointed out. 'Two years ago all that land grew a sparse crop of wheat or a few potatoes, much of it was not worked at all. Now they grow sugar cane, oranges and lemons, and in a few weeks some of the fields will look like sheets of red flame when the pomegranates are in flower.'

'All due to irrigation?' she queried.

'All due to one of my irrigation jobs,' he answered smugly.

'I see. Making the desert blossom like the rose.'

'That's better than creating dust-bowls,' he retorted.

'Of course.' She did not grudge him his self-satisfaction, for it was obvious how much a prosperous, fertile countryside meant to him. She contrasted his attitude with that of Paul and Don Ramiro, who desired nothing better than to make money out of commercialising a small coastal town.

'How long will you be on your new job at Zaragoza?' she asked after a mile or so.

'A year. Maybe two. Depends on how things go.'

'Then you'll be off elsewhere? Do you go to any other country apart from Spain?'

'Not yet. My firm has special interests in Spain and works in with the Government. It also trains Spanish technicians in England for a few months so that they can learn the latest developments in canal schemes and hydro-electric works.'

'You don't go back to England for holidays?'

His face became sombre. 'No. When I have holidays I spend them in some other part of Spain. Once or twice I've been to Portugal.'

Caran realised that he had shut a door in her face. She was not to probe into his life before coming to Spain. Although she took the hint and asked no further questions, he maintained conversation for the rest of the journey on an impersonal level.

He had to park his car on the outskirts of Murcia, for dense crowds prevented him from finding space.

'I don't know how we shall get through this mob,' he muttered when he and Caran walked towards the town centre. He took her hand and pulled her down a side street where there was less congestion. 'We'll cut off a corner this way,' he told her, 'unless we find ourselves blocked at the other end.'

Progress was impeded by strings of people coming the opposite way, but eventually Brooke and Caran came out on to a *paseo* by the river.

'We'll go farther along if we can,' he said. 'Better view.'

People were already standing six or seven deep along the street, but Caran obeyed Brooke's directions and hurried by his side. Now they were on a terraced embankment with gardens below.

'We should see the main procession coming towards us,' he explained, 'on its way to the Cathedral.'

He had timed the occasion well, for in a few minutes the first of the huge floats appeared, accompanied by brown-robed penitents.

Caran took out her notebook. 'Do you want to dictate notes, or shall I write down my own impressions?'

'Both,' he answered, as he unslung his camera. 'I'll give you some of the details. You can add others which I may miss.'

He took several photographs, then began dictation. 'Costumes of special interest—purple silk tunics only knee-length, so that they can show off their white woollen embroidered stockings. Special designs only found in this district and handed down through generations, like the costumes, as long as they will last.'

When he paused Caran glanced up from her shorthand notes to observe this great fiesta of colour and ceremony, pomp and an almost naïve rusticity.

'Many of the Nazarenes seem to have large rounded paunches,' she remarked. 'Surprising when you see how lean their faces are.'

Brooke laughed. 'That's their lunch under their tunics. They carry enough to share with their colleagues who support the floats. Now here comes the best float of all. The Last Supper.'

Caran realised how eager Brooke had been to add this lovely Murcian fiesta to his collection. The float was the largest Caran had ever seen, for it carried images of Christ and the twelve apostles seated at a long table, laid for supper.

'The food looks almost real,' she whispered.

'It is real,' Brooke answered. 'Twenty-six Nazarenes carry this float, and on Easter Sunday they'll all come to the house of the chief bearer and eat the food.'

Caran was entranced by this spectacle. A roll in the centre of a lace-edged napkin was placed in front of Christ, with a chalice and at some distance a whole roast lamb on a huge dish. Three large cooked fishes were set on each plate for the apostles. There was bread, lettuces and honey. The fruit was arranged in glowing patterns, figs, melons, green and black olives, apples, tomatoes.

'Why doesn't it fall off?' Caran asked, fearful lest with the involuntary jogging and swaying of the bearers, disaster should happen to the food.

'It's all wired down to the plates,' Brooke explained. 'One family has the privilege of buying all the food and displaying it; the job is passed down from father to son. Another man takes on the task of fixing it to the plates. Someone else looks after the cutlery, but all of them must be actual bearers. There's none of this sponsoring by the wealthy who can put their hands in their pockets, but stand aside in admiration while others do the hard work.'

By the time the processions were over, Caran was both tired and hungry, for she had eaten nothing since an early breakfast of coffee and rolls. She was glad when Brooke suggested that they must fight their way back to his car, where he had a picnic lunch.

'It would be senseless to try to eat in a restaurant today,' he said. 'At least, senseless for us. Everywhere is already full.'

'A credit mark for thoughtfulness,' she said lightly. 'I'm hungry.'

'I'm aware that most girls become irritable when they're needing a little refreshment.'

In his car they sat on the back seat and enjoyed cold roast chicken and tomatoes, with a bottle of wine, and little cakes.

Later in the afternoon when the streets were not so thronged Brooke took her to see the beautiful cathedral.

'One of the loveliest in all Spain,' murmured Brooke. 'Stone rising in a flight of architecture. Look at it long enough and it really does seem to move.'

Caran agreed with him as she gazed on the red-gold façade soaring tier upon tier with fluted columns supporting more columns above and winged angels riding the curves.

'Almost theatrical,' commented Caran. 'As though it were supported from behind.'

'It's handsome in sunlight, but unbelievable by moonlight.'

Some warm reminiscent flavour in his voice forced her to wonder in whose company he had stood here in the moonlight.

The town still held much of its original Moorish atmosphere and Caran never tired of wandering around the narrow streets or coming unexpectedly to part of the old walls, with one of the innumerable watch-towers.

'We'll go back through Lorca,' he suggested. 'Then we can have dinner there at a reasonable time.'

She realised how little she had explored the district, for she had to admit that she had not visited Lorca.

Brooke tut-tutted. 'I don't know what you've done with your time here. Have you enjoyed the winter?'

Caran was thoughtful. 'It's been interesting,' she said at last.

'Only interesting?' he queried.

She longed to tell him that the part of winter she had found most stimulating was up to the end of January when he had left Albarosa, but she would not admit that she had missed him.

'We've had ups and downs,' she said now. 'Delays with the villas and so on.'

'But everything is marvellous now and you're all set for a glorious summer?'

'Yes,' she agreed quickly, for in her mind she saw the long warm summer stretch before her as an arid desert without Brooke to enliven or nettle her by turns.

When they were seated in a restaurant in Lorca and he had ordered dinner, he returned to the subject.

'Have you found out any more about the developments Paul has in mind?' he asked.

Caran now saw no need for caution. She told Brooke briefly of the disclosures Paul and his aunt had made. 'A charming little holiday village,' she said bitterly. 'Hotels, shops, cafés, swimming pool, night clubs, the lot. And between those two men I've been nothing but a catspaw.'

'I suspected something like this a year ago. A man like Paul would never let such a good opportunity slip. That's one reason why he was delighted when I had to leave my villa. Naturally, he didn't want a sitting tenant stuck there.'

Caran looked across the table at Brooke. 'Mrs. Parmenter was also delighted with your absence.' She grinned. 'Untidy, gave the place a disreputable look, she said. A proper lout.'

His blue eyes danced. 'You're making it up!' he accused.

She shook her head. 'No. Her exact words—almost. I added the word "lout", but that's what she really meant.'

'Does it make a difference to you?' he asked later when they had finished the meal and were on the way out to the car. 'All these plans, pulling down and putting up.'

'I shall see how things go,' she said vaguely.

Yet on the journey towards the coast and the little fishing village of Matana, he asked further questions about her future. It seemed as though he could not leave the subject alone.

'Has Paul offered you any kind of security?' he wanted to know. 'What happens to you when the hotel is open and the villas are being demolished?'

She sighed. 'That's a long way ahead, so Mrs. Parmenter tells me. I can see that for myself. One can't wave a magic wand and see a hotel rising floor by floor. But Paul speaks of giving me any department I want to run.'

'And that isn't what you want?'

Caran looked ahead through the windscreen. 'I don't know.' She did not know what prompted her to say the next words, for they seemed to tumble out of their own accord. 'If I wanted security, I suppose I could always accept Don Ramiro's offer.'

'And what offer is that?' he queried in a cool, crisp voice.

'Marriage,' she said flatly.

She had imagined that his immediate reaction would be a loud guffaw, a scornful comment—'So you've hooked him at last!' or something like that.

Instead, he said quietly, 'I wondered when you would tell me about that or if you were keeping it a dark secret.'

'How did you know?' she demanded.

'I have a very efficient spy system in Albarosa. Not much happens there that I don't know about.' After a long pause, he asked, 'And are you accepting Don Ramiro's handsome offer?'

'Does it concern you?'

'In a way, yes. Don Ramiro would be very surprised if you did. He doesn't mean it. Oh, he may pretend that he's captivated and all that, but it's all part of the scheme to make

174

you feel important and cherished. He and Paul have been hoping to win you over to their ideas. They still need some-one like you to manage the villas.'

'There would be Julie if she wants to stay,' Caran suggested.

'Not the same. Julie would neglect her duties at the drop of a hat, especially if the hat belonged to an attractive well-heeled man. You're different. Your conscience gets in the way.'

Caran smiled. 'My conscience must be dormant today.'

'Why?'

'I refused to go to Granada with Don Ramiro. Then I've played truant without telling Paul that I was coming to Murcia with you.'

'I must count myself flattered,' he returned drily.

'Unintentional on my part.'

'Flattery is the last thing I'd expect from you, my dear Caran.'

'You're smug enough without any help from me,' she retorted.

He remained silent for a long time, but Caran did not delude herself that his silence was due to her last remark. Brooke was not so easily quelled.

When he was driving down the road to the villas he said, 'We're invited to supper at Felipe and Gabriela's tomorrow night.'

'We? Is it a party?'

'No. Just us. Will you come?'

Although his words sounded casual enough she detected an underlying note of appeal. No, that was too strong a word. Better to say that he had a reason for wanting her to accept.

'Yes, I'll come,' she agreed. 'Thank you for taking me to Murcia. I enjoyed it.' She waited a moment before sliding out of the car when he stopped. If she had expected a wild embrace, an affectionate hug or even a fleeting good night kiss, she was disappointed. He was staring straight ahead of him, his hands on the steering wheel.

'Good night, Caran,' he murmured. 'Come to Gabriela's about nine.'

He spun the car on the gravel parking area and shot off up the road to the town.

As she let herself in her villa, her thoughts meandered back over the day's events. Enjoyable though it had been, she scolded herself for a fool. Brooke's reappearance after more than two months' absence was more than enough to re-awaken those hopeless longings, that attraction that drew her towards the one man who had no use for her except as a pleasant car-companion on a day trip. The only comforting factor was the knowledge that she would see him tomorrow.

CHAPTER TEN

PAUL greeted Caran next morning with an obvious lack of cordiality. 'I'm sorry you didn't change your mind and go to Granada yesterday.'

'I went to Murcia instead.'

'So I gather. With Eldridge.'

'Yes.' Caran saw no reason to lie.

Paul shook his head sadly. 'A pity. Don Ramiro won't like to hear that you turned down his invitation and then went off in the opposite direction with another man.'

'How much control over my life has Don Ramiro?' she asked. 'I'm not engaged to him.'

'I wish to heaven you were!' Paul spoke with intense feeling.

Caran smiled. 'Don't worry, Paul. I didn't neglect the guests. If I'd gone to Granada the day before I wouldn't have been here to settle them in properly. Besides, you don't have to tell Don Ramiro every little detail. I shan't inform him.'

He walked moodily along the path with her. 'You don't realise how important it is to keep on the right side of that man.'

'You can do that admirably. As for me, I don't really count in the end. I'm only an employee.'

'But our most important one,' Paul assured her. He talked about several small details concerning the lettings, then asked suddenly, 'You're not thinking of getting married to that chap Eldridge, are you?'

Caran laughed. 'So far he hasn't asked me, and I doubt if he ever would. He's not the marrying kind.'

'That's all right, then.' Paul sighed with relief. 'I'd hate to think of losing you to that footloose mudlark.'

Caran reflected that it was in some measure thanks to such footloose mudlarks, Spanish as well as a sprinkling of English, that Albarosa and its surroundings owed its fertility and much of its livelihood in fruit-growing, apart from an adequate water supply. She knew that at one time Albarosa could be approached only by tracks across dry river beds until a better road was built. Now the rivers were harnessed high up in the hills, their torrents controlled.

After a few moments she said aloud, 'I'd better tell you that I'm meeting Brooke tonight. We're having a meal with that couple who were here with their children in Cristal.'

'Oh?' Paul was not interested in the Ribera family. 'But of course I didn't mean to criticise how you spend your spare time,' he added quickly.

'Brooke is only here for a day or so,' Caran informed him. 'After that he'll be off again to his mudlarking.'

Paul smoothed his fair hair. 'There ought to be a few attractive young men staying here during the summer, so that you could enjoy a little fun.'

Caran nodded absently. Paul meant to be kind, but she had no intention of acting a handy available girl for chance visitors. The men must find their partners in flirtation among the other guests. Caran refused to be classed as part of the service, but there was no point in telling Paul.

She worked hard during the day, not forgetting to type notes of the fiesta yesterday so that she could give them to Brooke tonight.

He met her outside the shop where the Riberas lived over the top. He grasped her wrist and pulled her towards the windows stacked with leather wallets and handbags as well as a saddle or two. There were pieces of wrought iron, decorative hanging baskets for patios; fancy pottery and serviceable cups and saucers.

'The man who owns this shop is an expert castanet-maker,' murmured Brooke. 'How would you like a pair?'

'But I wouldn't know how to use them,' she objected, and was immediately contrite at this brusque rebuff. What impelled her to look Brooke's gift-horse in the mouth?

'You can learn, can't you?' he demanded testily. 'Benita would teach you.'

She was inside the shop almost without knowing it and Brooke was being shown dozens of pairs of castanets.

'Edmundo makes castanets for all the well-known flamenco artists,' Brooke told Caran, while he expertly clicked a pair with his fingers. 'It's not easy, you know. Each pair takes two or three days to make.'

'*Si, si,*' put in Edmundo. 'One must choose the wood carefully. See? The grain must run this way.' He held a pair of the polished mussel-shaped instruments in his hands. 'Then when you have made them, you file them until you get the clear sound.'

'This looks a good pair,' suggested Brooke, picking up another couple.

'Perhaps.' Edmundo, a burly, elderly man whose fleshy hands were yet smooth and sensitive, cast a fleeting upward glance at Brooke. Then he turned towards a shelf with small boxes. 'Here is a special pair,' he said, opening the lid of a box. 'Very pretty sound.'

Brooke picked them up, tried them and nodded. Edmundo then played them, strutting and jigging in flamenco style to his own rhythm.

As he wrapped up the parcel and handed it to Caran, Edmundo said, 'You will soon be able to click them. They will make much music for you.'

In the rooms above the shop, Gabriela and Felipe were waiting eagerly for their guests. Benita was also there with her mother Manuela.

'Not dancing tonight at the restaurant?' enquired Caran.

'Oh, yes, but too early,' replied Benita. 'I dance at half-past ten or eleven.'

Gabriela had provided a wonderfully tasty meal of a *zarzuela* of fish, the mixed fry so popular everywhere in Spain. Then followed little *tortillas*, omelettes with chopped potatoes and ham, finally a custard flan and fruit. There was adequate wine to drink and Caran suspected that Brooke had provided part of the feast.

Caran produced her newly-acquired castanets and they were much admired. Benita showed her how to hold them.

'You put your thumb through the loop and the first finger so. Now you play with the other fingers. When it is daytime, I will teach you,' she offered.

Gabriela added that too much noise would wake the children, who were asleep in the two adjoining bedrooms.

It was obvious to Caran that Gabriela and Felipe assumed that she and Brooke were rather more than just casual acquaintances. Their smiles, their happy looks as they raised their glasses all pointed to a bracketing that Caran knew did not exist.

When she and Brooke left just before midnight, Gabriela said softly, 'Señor Brooke is so kind. He is perhaps the kindest man I have ever known, except, of course, Felipe.'

The words were spoken as a strong recommendation, but Caran merely smiled and said nothing.

The streets were still alive with people, but the road down to the villas was deserted. Brooke walked along with Caran, but not touching her, and she saw their two shadows in the moonlight, separated by a strip of pale roadway. She longed to close that gap, to be held in his arms, so that their shadows melted, yet she could do no more than trudge along her own path.

When they had almost reached the villas, Brooke suddenly flung away his cigar and the glowing tip rolled in the road. She was in his arms without further warning and he was kissing her mouth, her cheeks, her neck. This was no casual goodbye kiss, she knew, and she responded as she had never before reacted to any man.

'Caran!' he murmured. 'Oh, I wish it could be otherwise.'

She pulled away from him a little, although she was still encircled by his embrace.

'How—otherwise?' Her voice was no more than a whisper, for it was full of fear.

'You must forget me. We must forget each other. It wouldn't be fair on any woman—not the kind of life I have to lead.'

Now she had wholly withdrawn herself. 'I think I understand.' The effort she made to prevent a flood of tears made her voice unnaturally hard. 'You needn't explain, Brooke.'

'You don't really understand. Perhaps it is that I'm not the marrying kind.'

Not the marrying kind! The words she had used when

talking about him to Paul.

'There's nothing more to say,' she said in as level a voice as she could find. She meant quite the reverse. There was everything to say. She wanted to tell him that if he loved her even one-tenth as much as she loved him, she would live the rough life with him, wherever his work compelled him to go. Other women had endured hardships and made homes for men because love was there to provide an enveloping aura of happiness that compensated for lack of home comforts.

Gabriela and Felipe had made themselves content even when living in a stable. They had kept their faith and trust in each other until better accommodation came along.

Brooke had managed to live in a villa while working on a site in the hills behind Albarosa. Yet he would not now allow her to share what he could offer.

She was not aware of how long she and Brooke stood there in silence. When she glanced at his face she saw the stern, rugged lines of his features. With despair she turned away and began to walk the short distance to the villas.

In one stride he caught up with her, thrusting out his hand to grasp hers. She shook his hand away impatiently, although the touch of his fingers fired her to the point where she wanted to abandon all pretence and throw herself into his arms.

Perhaps other girls had done just that and he had whispered soothing words ... 'You'll soon get over it ... I should only make you unhappy'—that sort of mush.

At the door of her villa she turned towards him. Now he was silhouetted against the moonlight and she could not see more than the blur of his face.

'Goodbye, Brooke,' she muttered in a low, furious voice. 'Don't try to see me again. It's finished. You need not spare me another thought when you pick up your next girl. After all, by now you must have had plenty of practice in forgetting.'

He stood motionless like a statue carved in bronze.

Blinded now by tears, she fumbled for her key, dithered it in the lock until at last the door opened. Even now at this last minute she realised that she had been hoping that he would rush to the door to help her, take her in his arms, kiss away her tears and assure her that he loved her and some time in the future might marry her.

But as she turned to close the door she saw his shadow still there, immovable, unwavering.

In her bedroom she sat for a long time, frozen, unable to think clearly. How easy it was for him to form these casual friendships, then break them when it suited him! She undressed and slid into bed, but not to sleep. Her strong determination came to the rescue of her weakness. If he could forget, so could she. No longer would the memory of his embrace cause her to buckle at the knees. She would live her life as though she had never met Brooke Eldridge.

When Julie returned from her visit to Malaga she asked, 'And what gaieties did you have here?'

'Brooke turned up for a day or two and took me to Murcia for a fiesta,' Caran answered with a superb self-control.

'Fine! Where now? Back to his hide-out in the north?'

'Yes, I think so.'

'Any news of the gallant Don?' queried Julie.

'Not as far as I know,' replied Caran. She was relieved when apparently Julie was satisfied not to probe for further disclosures.

In April several of the villas became occupied for a fortnight or so at a time. The two new ones, Perla and Diamante, were popular because of their wonderful position on the far side of the little spit of land.

'Let's make the most of those two,' advised Paul one day to Caran, 'while we have the chance. Soon it will be all noise and dust when the hotel is being built.'

Surprisingly, Caran found herself taking a much greater interest in all the new projects of development. Paul had shown her plans and artist's impressions of the layout when finished, and she had to admit that it all looked attractive if what you wanted was a delightful village by the sea.

She had succeeded in pushing all thoughts of Brooke not quite out of her mind, for that was impossible, but into the farthest crevices. She had even become accustomed to passing or entering his Villa Zafiro without a pang of memory.

Mrs. Parmenter returned to England in May, but promised to revisit the villas before the autumn.

'And do think again of what I advised,' were her parting words to Caran. 'About Paul. He needs good direction.'

Caran smiled non-committally, but reflected that Paul would never receive that good direction from her. He had taken a room at El Catalan in order to leave all the villas free and Julie had vacated Esmeralda and rented a small flat on the advice of Señora Molina, to whom Caran had introduced her.

Caran stayed in her own Villa Joyosa so that she was usually on the spot.

During the summer months she found it easy to take time off for an hour or so in the day and often spent it swimming in the clear water or lazing on the sandy shore. Sometimes Julie joined her, for they had a special little part of the beach and their own straw wigwam shade.

One afternoon Julie raised herself on one elbow and asked suddenly, 'Do you ever hear anything of Brooke?'

'No. Why should I? I don't know his address. He's probably moved on somewhere else by now.' Caran remembered how several days after the visit to Murcia she had found in her handbag the typed notes of the fiesta. She had intended to give them to Brooke at Gabriela's house, but she had forgotten them. She put the pages in an envelope and gave it to Benita to send on. No letter. He did not need that.

Now Julie changed the subject and spoke of a family of guests in one of the villas. Caran was never quite sure how much Julie suspected or whether she eventually intended to mark him down for her own. In that case, she would need to know how far Caran was involved.

'It's a bit thick,' Julie was saying now, 'how some of these people come from England and expect the maid to work eighteen hours a day for them, fetching and carrying. I pointed out to this lot that the girls work thirty hours a week and no more. "Oh, we can pay for overtime," says this large, fat mum sprawling in her long chair.'

Caran giggled at this description of the stout woman referred to. 'Money talks, but it doesn't always speak Spanish,' she said.

'People who are accustomed to maids at home—whoever they may be in these servantless days——' continued Julie, 'always treat them with respect. It's these jumped-up lots who clean their own kitchen floors who are so demanding.'

'Like the ones who want their fridges re-stocked free of charge,' Caran put in with a laugh.

She and Julie had originally laughed their heads off when earlier in the season a woman had told Caran quite sharply that the food stocks were practically exhausted.

'The fridge is practically empty,' she complained. 'I should have thought it was part of your organisation to see that we have enough food.'

'But you must order whatever you want,' Caran pointed out. 'You'll see that according to the brochure, we supply you with about two days' food and drink to give you a start. You wouldn't expect to go shopping immediately you arrived, would you?'

'You mean we now have to *pay* for what we order?' demanded the guest.

'Of course. You are renting a villa here. It's not a hotel.'

After that episode Caran had been extremely careful to impress upon visitors that after the initial free supply, they bought or ordered their own food and drink.

With the influx of different parties of people Caran had found a slight easing of that dull ache which never seemed to leave her. One day she had been turning out a drawer in her dressing-table and come across the box with the castanets that Brooke had given her. Since that night of parting she had never opened it. Now she took out the little polished pieces and it was then that she saw in tiny gilded letters on each pair, 'To Caran'. All the longing and loneliness welled up in her, threatening her peace of mind.

So Brooke had been in league with Edmundo, pretending to choose a pair of castanets at random when both men had known that a specially-inscribed pair was waiting in a box.

Yet another parting gift, thought Caran. Spain and perhaps other places must be full of girls hugging little farewell treasures. From Brooke—but not with his love. She replaced the castanets in the drawer. She would never learn to play them now.

August was a crowded month, all the villas were full and Caran had little free time. Paul had set up a small temporary bar in a corner of the gardens facing the sea. Half a dozen tables, a few chairs, glasses and an array of bottles provided a meeting place for the guests if they wanted to spend an hour or so talking to companions. 'It saves them traipsing up into the town if they don't want to go that far,' was Paul's view. 'A youth of eighteen or so to serve drinks and look after the tables ought not to cost much for labour.'

There was no doubt, Caran often thought, that Paul was quick to see people's needs and do his best to cater for them. As Julie had once said, Paul would certainly end up in the hotel tycoon category.

Caran and Paul were sitting at a table one evening when he spoke of Julie.

'If only I knew where I stood with her! I thought when she first came here that she liked me and that I might stand a chance, but she's like a piece of quicksilver. You can't ever pin her down.'

'Be patient, Paul,' she advised him. 'Julie's not the type to be pinned down unless she's quite sure that's what she wants and then she prefers to do the pinning. Give her time and perhaps one day everything will come right for you.'

'I'm at a tricky stage in my career just now, but in a year or so I'd have something quite substantial to offer her.'

'Julie has tremendous confidence in you, if that's any comfort,' Caran assured him.

After a long silence during which he communed with his wine, he said, 'What about you, Caran? I've wondered if you really liked that chap Eldridge. Did you?'

The semi-darkness hid any colour that flushed her cheeks and she answered coolly, 'Oh, I liked him in some ways. I've almost forgotten about him now.'

'It's been a good summer.' Paul was speaking now of the material side. 'We've shown a substantial profit and can well justify the financial deal we made about the villas.'

A good summer! Caran had so looked forward to it, but it had been ashes. Brooke had said he wished he could be in Albarosa for the summer, but he hadn't meant it.

'Now is the summer of my discontent,' she misquoted to herself. It was the winter and then spring that Brooke had made exciting. Winter would come again, but it would not bring Brooke.

Towards the end of August there was to be a special display of flamenco in a cave near Albarosa, so Benita informed Caran.

'We have this every year,' Benita said, 'with many good dancers and singers. You must come.'

'Of course,' agreed Caran. 'Perhaps I could bring a few of our visitors, too?'

'Naturally. We must have a good audience.'

Caran took the precaution of inspecting the cave beforehand. She did not want complaints about shoes being ruined stumbling about on rough boulders. She found the approach not too difficult and made up a party of guests for the appointed evening, and arranged the necessary transport.

It was dark when the cars set out and already Caran was wishing she had never agreed to conduct such a party, for the road from Albarosa to the adjacent hill would be unlit as well as fairly rough.

Her fears were unfounded, for young lads lined the route with torches and the effect was that of a procession of wavering fireflies.

In the cave, chairs were set out, the floor sanded and dry with a boarded platform for the dancers. Caran settled her party in their places and hoped they would think the performance worth the journey.

There were songs first, very noisy and gay, to warm up the atmosphere. Two guitarists played accompaniments aided by a *bandurria*, a metal-stringed instrument, startling in its volume.

Then the dancers followed with their frenzied roll of the hips, the rattling of castanets and high heels, the sinuous bending and posturing of the body. The audience became more excited, emphasising the rhythms with hand-clapping.

Caran found herself becoming absorbed into the spirit of the songs and dances. She glanced away from the improvised stage through the smoke-filled, lantern-lit scene and, for an instant, imagined that she saw Brooke on the far side of the cave. But of course it was an illusion.

Eventually the show was over and the audience, some of them still a little dazed, filed out.

Benita came over to Caran. 'Was it good?' she asked.

'Marvellous. And you danced as well as any of the others.'

This was a compliment that Benita appreciated, for she had been in competition tonight with quite well-known and more experienced dancers from other districts.

Caran shepherded her party to their cars and was about to enter Paul's when an arm thrust around her waist dragged her away.

'I'll bring Caran,' a voice barked in her ear.

She needed neither lantern nor torch to identify the owner.

'Let me go!' she muttered in a low, furious tone. 'What do you think you're——'

Brooke clapped a hand over her mouth and drew her farther away from the thinning crowd. His arm was like an iron clamp and her struggles ceased.

'Now!' he said harshly when the last stragglers were disappearing. He still held her so firmly that she would have found it difficult to free herself.

'Perhaps you'll explain this rough handling,' she said.

His arms relaxed and she twisted away from his grasp, but he held her captive by the wrist.

'Tell me the truth, Caran. Is it worth anything to you that I've come back—even in this dramatic manner?'

'Whether you come or stay away doesn't mean anything to me,' she snapped. Her heart cried out that the words were not true, but she refused to let him burden her yet again with that aching anguish she had suffered for so many months.

'You mean something to me,' he said, his voice vibrant.

For a moment she thought she detected a faint gleam of hope, but she crushed it down. 'Yes. Just another girl in Spain, a companion for a few months. And then—goodbye.'

'Not this time, Caran darling. I'm never going to say goodbye to you again. I've had to come back for you. I couldn't stay away. You've ruined my life.'

'I? Ruined *your* life?' In her incredulity she was unaware of how much stress she had put on that word 'your'.

'Yes. And I'm glad.' He held her in his arms and kissed her cheek. 'All the time I've been in Spain I swore I'd never get too involved with any girl. My life for the next year or two isn't the wine and roses sort that any girl could fancy. But you—you turned it inside out. You flirted with Paul. You threw Don Ramiro in my face. I was so damned jealous that I could hardly look at you without wanting to pick you up and carry you off up to the mountains.'

'Like Angelina's brigand?' She had regained a little of her confidence, remembering the girl at the mountain inn.

'Worse. Even he earned a smile from her. I received nothing from you except a stony, cold indifference.'

'I was never cold or indifferent,' she contradicted.

'Then let's put that to the test.' With his lips on hers, demanding, yet not wounding, she knew the joy of yielding without that haunting fear that the rapturous moment was only transient.

'Now do I mean anything to you?' he wanted to know.

'Perhaps. A little.'

'I want more than that. I went away because I loved you so much that I couldn't bear to break your heart. When I took on that job, which I'd asked for to put distance between us, I still loved you and it was breaking my own heart. Now, are you going to marry me?'

'I expect so.'

'Why?' he queried, dabbing a kiss on her eyebrow.

She sighed. 'Because I suppose I'm crazy, have no sense and—woe is me—I love you.'

After a while a voice in the darkness called, 'Señor Brooke? Do you come?'

'Yes, Benita. I come and Caran comes.'

Benita emerged from the shadows where she had evidently been patiently waiting for Brooke to take her home.

In the car he said, 'Benita has been my true and trusty spy

all the time.'

Caran laughed. 'You needed a spy since you didn't trust me with your address.'

'I couldn't trust myself to write to you,' he replied.

'I wondered sometimes if I ought to be jealous of Benita.' Caran turned to smile at the girl in the back of the car.

Brooke grunted. 'Benita has a handsome *novio* of her own. She'd never look twice at me.' He translated for Benita's benefit.

'I wonder why *I* did,' sighed Caran.

'You were stopped in your tracks when you first clapped eyes on me,' he retorted happily, and began to sing a gay Spanish song with a gypsy flavour.

Benita alighted outside her own house and shyly put her hand into Caran's. 'You must always be happy now. Your man has come to you.'

'*Gracias*, Benita. *Muchas gracias*,' replied Caran.

'When do you have to return to Zaragoza?' she asked Brooke outside her own villa.

'Not for a few days. I'm staying in the town with some Spanish friends. I moved heaven and earth to get myself transferred to Zaragoza. Now I'm demanding to be allowed to come back nearer here and work on the irrigation project north of Murcia. Even that's too far away for my liking. I shall have to invent a scheme for Albarosa itself.'

Julie took the news calmly when Caran told her next day.

'I've seen it coming a mile away. If you're ecstatic about him, then I'm glad. You could do better for yourself, of course, but at least I shan't have to keep my weather eye open if someone I really fancy comes along.'

'Oh, rubbish, Julie. You're not that much of a gold-digger just for the sake of the gold.'

'Try me!' retorted Julie, as she kissed Caran. 'Be happy with him, pet. He's not too bad.' After a few moments she added, 'I'd have a cut at Don Ramiro if I thought it worth while, but now that we hear rumours of his impending engagement to the dark beauty Mirella, all is lost for me in that direction.'

Paul was concerned lest Caran should want to leave her work immediately. 'I knew that man was a menace right from the start. Still, best wishes all the same,' he added belatedly.

Caran assured him that she would remain for some long time yet, for Brooke had to wait for his transfer to Murcia.

Surprisingly, it was Don Ramiro who insisted on giving a dinner party at the Marroqui for Caran and Brooke. Paul and Julie were naturally invited and, compared with some of those other occasions, this was an amicable affair, with none of the warring undercurrents.

In a quiet moment Don Ramiro said to Caran, 'I hope we shall always remain friends.'

'Of course,' agreed Caran quickly. 'I should not like to lose your friendship.'

'My betrothal to my cousin Mirella will soon be announced when the details have been settled, but the news is not yet public.'

'I understand. Congratulations.'

On the other side of her Brooke was complaining that he could see only the back of her head, charming though it was.

Don Ramiro smiled and proposed a toast. 'In Spain we have a proverb that it is better to begin a friendship with a little aversion. Perhaps that has been true in the case of our two friends here.' The toasts were drunk, Benita gave a special performance and at the end bowed several times to Don Ramiro's table.

Paul agreed that Caran could take all the free time she wanted while Brooke was here, and next day Brooke took her in his car along some of the less frequented roads in the hills behind Albarosa.

They had both brought ample picnic lunches. 'Evidently we were afraid of starving,' commented Brooke, laughing.

'I'm told there's a Spanish proverb which says that love is a furnace but it will not cook the stew,' Caran returned.

'Oh, I can probably outdo you in Spanish proverbs any day,' he boasted. 'Listen to this one and take heed. They say, "If your wife tells you to throw yourself from a balcony, pray

God that it's a low one." I shall take care when it comes to choosing an apartment in Murcia that we're not on the top floor.'

They spoke of the future, of visits to England to meet Caran's parents and Brooke's father and two married brothers. They sat dreaming in the shade of pine trees on a sloping hillside and when the afternoon faded into evening Brooke brought her to the ruins of the old Mendosa castle, pale red-gold in the slanting sunshine.

There was not much left of the castle now except the remains of two towers and a long piece of wall enclosing what had once been a courtyard.

Caran and Brooke leaned against the crumbling stone, gazed at the purple sea glinting pink and gold where the sun caught it. 'I've wanted to bring you here—so that we could both tread where once the mighty Mendosas trod.'

She turned to watch the sun drop behind the mauve hills, while still casting a dusky pink glow on the white Moorish houses of Albarosa.

'It's true what Don Ramiro said,' murmured Caran softly. 'Spain claims you. If you leave you feel drawn back again.'

'Even in winter when the rain in Spain does *not* fall mainly in the plain?'

'Even in winter. This was the summer of my discontent.'

'And mine,' he agreed. 'Now made glorious by——?'

'When summer comes to Albarosa it stays all the year round if the right person is in the right place.'

'I said you were a philosopher.' He hugged her to him as they walked back to the car.

The distant mountains faded to blue haze, the valleys in shadow now purple as a grape, but a final gleam of rosy pink picked out the topmost tower of Albarosa, a place of summer in the heart.

Have You Missed Any of These Harlequin Romances?